# A COUNTRY CHRISTMAS

## A FARMER'S LOVE
### BOOK TWO

LILLIANA ROSE

# BLURB

Zoe has taken the biggest risk of her life. She's moved in with Max on his farm, to see if she can have a future with a man she'd only met months ago. A man who is arrogant, and downright selfish at times.

As an edgy legal secretary, Zoe can match his sharp tongue, which only adds to the attraction between them. But is life with Max on the farm really her future?

Max is trying to adjust to having Zoe in his life and doesn't want to mess things up. She's given up everything to be with him, but so far he hasn't made any sacrifices.

Can a bachelor who's stuck in his ways, learn to let the woman he loves into his life, and secure a future for their family?

# A COUNTRY CHRISTMAS

*To my dog, Astro.*
*You are a star in the sky,*
*but it's not the same*
*as having you by my feet*
*when I'm writing.*

# INFORMATION AND DICTIONARY

This book has been written using US English, but the book's story is set in Australia. Some euphemisms that form part of the Australian spoken word may be used. If you would like further explanation, or to discuss Australia, please do not hesitate to contact the author. Contact details have been provided, for your convenience, at the end of this book.

# CHAPTER 1

"Where's my breakfast?"

The backdoor slammed.

Bluey whimpered at not being allowed inside the house.

Zoe took a bite of her strawberry jam on toast when Max walked in. He had thick, blue woolen socks on his feet, wearing dusty blue work pants, and a checked shirt, undone at the top revealing his chest. He'd been out to do the morning jobs on his farm, Greenfields. His comment grated on her feminist beliefs, but that faded with the cheeky grin he gave her, which lightened up his dark eyes with a smoldering heat that sent sparks firing between her legs.

*Will I ever get used to his inappropriate comments?*

With a bun in the oven, she felt like she had to. Or

1

at least give it a try. She was heading toward three months pregnant, after they had a hot one-night stand at the Royal Adelaide Show back at the start of spring. Max was the father and it had messed up her plans.

At twenty-five she had been wholly focussed on building her career as a legal secretary, not trying to work out if she was going to breastfeed or bottle-feed or if she could change a nappy. Let alone be able to adjust to life on a cattle farm—one where the closest neighbor was about five miles away—with a babe in arms. Her belly fluttered, and it wasn't the baby turning, the nerves were getting worse, and it was becoming harder to ignore them.

*If only Mom and Dad would come and visit for Christmas, or her friends, Ellie and Billie.*

"You weren't here, so I threw it in the bin." She looked at him coolly, trying to keep the humor from her facial expression, her comment firing straight back at his without missing a beat. She could match him, she knew it, and she used it to her full advantage. Well, at least she tried.

Max was thirty-four, and the age difference had never been an issue between them. At least it was one thing that Zoe knew wouldn't be the cause of them not working out. It was early days yet. They had known each other as long as the baby had grown inside of her. It wasn't long enough to have packed up her life in Adelaide to move in with a man she didn't know. But for the sake of the baby she had. Of course, there was an attraction there too, and somehow the fiery relationship they had appealed to them both.

He held his hand to his heart. "You hurt me deep."

"As if."

"Now, now, don't be like that on a lazy summer Sunday morning. Especially when Christmas is in twenty-five days." He raised his eyebrow suggestively as he walked toward her. "I'll just let you know that I'm hoping for a special gift from you when I wake up Christmas morning."

Zoe squirmed in her seat as she felt her lower abdominal muscles clench with need. "Well, now that will depend if you're naughty or nice."

"Good thing I know exactly how to balance naughty and nice for your full pleasure." Max stood next to Zoe, leaning against the 1960s-style kitchen table with chrome legs and edging which gave it an odd space-age look.

A bolt of desire coursed through her body. She could feel his heat radiating around her and she knew exactly what his intentions were. His masculine scent sent her mind wild with anticipation. Inhaling slowly, she met his gaze, his dark eyes burned with lust.

*Fuck.* She found it hard to resist him. It didn't help that sparks flew between them so easily, which resulted in her getting pregnant in the first place. The connection between them was built on lust, attraction, and sex, which caused them to lose themselves in the moment of passion. She was also all too well aware that these points were not at all the solid foundation for a future relationship, and yet here they were attempting just that.

*Damn hormones.* She couldn't resist him even if she wanted to. This fact was made a hundred times harder with her raging hormones, much to Max's amusement and delight.

Zoe leaned back in her chair. She felt a little guilty only having gotten out of bed not that long ago, when Max had been up early working on the farm. Pregnant or not, she wanted to pull her weight and do her share of the workload. At least, while she still could. Give it a few months, when she would be waddling around with a huge pregnant belly, that might be different. Now, it was a tight little bump, and it wasn't getting in the way of anything.

"Do you now?" Zoe raised her bare leg and put her foot suggestively on the edge of the table. She wore her pajamas—floral cotton shorts with a tight pink tank top—they were one of her favorites from the designer Peter Alexander.

He smirked. Ran his finger down the side of her bare leg which was up on the table next to him.

She inhaled sharply. *Fuck, yes, he did.* She enjoyed the way her skin prickled under his touch as his hand moved up her thigh, coming closer to where she really wanted him to touch her, that place where he could get her juices flowing.

"Though, if you're not up for it," he said softly, his hand pausing on her thigh.

Her desires flamed almost out of control. "What on earth gave you that impression?"

Max chuckled. "You're in your pajamas after all, and it's nearly nine."

"It's Sunday morning," she reminded him. "You're meant to stay in bed for this to happen."

"I better make up for it now."

A shiver of pleasure ran through her—she quite liked the sound of that.

Max leaned forward and kissed her. His lips pushing hers open as if eager to taste her fully. He glided his hand under her shorts, fingers brushing high under her thigh.

Zoe looked square in his eyes, daring him to go further. Instead, he pulled his hand away. She was about to protest, when he suddenly reached down, hands around her waist, basically picked her up, turned and perched her on the edge of the table. She naturally wrapped her legs around his waist, pulling him closer her. She could feel his cock hardened even behind the material. She tilted her hips back, suggestively, rubbing against him, feeling what she really wanted to be inside of her.

Max's hands slipped under the back of her top, massaging upward, gliding over her skin, his touch sending her temperature rising with desire. "That's better, I can feel more of you this way."

His lips found hers once more, they danced over her mouth, his tongue flicking over hers. She moaned with delight into the kiss, enjoying the feel of his hands on her back, pressing her closer into him.

He bunched up her top, the soft material gliding over her skin easily, pushed it up over her head, then he let it fall to the floor. Soft sounds escaped his lips while he gazed at her as if he was drinking up her partly naked body. His hands moved quickly up over her shoulders, then down her bare arms, under her ribs, finally stopping as they cupped her breasts. She felt her nipples harden as his fingers massaged her soft flesh, teasing the lust between them toward feverishly hot. Her back arched backward, her chest forward, giving him full access to pleasure her. He moved, pressed his mouth over her breast, then he sucked gently. Letting his teeth graze over her sensitive nipple, he then pulled away which caused her to breathe in sharply with pleasure. He did the same to her other nipple, and she felt the juices pool heavily between her leg.

Urgency grew between them, her intimate muscles clenched wanting him to enter her. His breath heavy on her neck as he embraced her. Using both hands, he lifted her just enough from the table, pulled down her pajama shorts sliding them down her legs.

In a flurry of necessity, she reached out, undid his work pants, pushed them down along with his jocks, releasing his hard, hot cock. He moved back between her legs. His cock slipped in her thick juices. Gliding up and down her length, he took time to tease her for longer.

She whimpered softly, closed her eyes as pleasure tingled her body. She was about to tell him to get the fuck into her, when she felt him move, his cock rested at her entrance. She flicked open her eyes, as if begging him. He pressed himself into her, his cock parting her tight muscles, which madly convulsed with pleasure. She groaned heavily, tilted her head back, closed her eyes, and let Max take her to the dizzying heights of an orgasm as he plunged in and out of her, building the tension expertly so it flooded over her in wave after wave. With a gasp, her body tipped over the edge as the tension broke. He moved once more in and out of her, keeping her buzzing with the pleasure, as he reached his own, spilling inside of her with passion. He wrapped his arms around her, as they breathed fast and heavy, the heat between them sparking.

Zoe nestled her head onto his shoulder. She felt the connection between them strengthen as they embraced, while they both enjoying the aftermath of their intimacy. If only they could spend the entire day like this. While she hadn't been living here on the farm with him for long, she had already realized that it didn't matter if it were a Sunday, some jobs couldn't wait. There would always be something that would drag Max back outside soon enough.

"You feel a little tense," said Max, his hands moving

up to her shoulders. "Perhaps I didn't show you how naughty I could be."

"Or maybe you need to show me how nice you can be." She gazed into his eyes.

Dare she hope that Max might have a little bit of time for her today. Even more than what he'd just given her just then, no matter how sated she'd felt.

"Just because it's nearly Christmas, how about I give you a massage?"

"Nothing to do with you loving me? Or that I'm carrying your child?"

"Our child." He rested his hand on her belly.

Zoe felt a bubbly movement. It was quick, fast, and nothing like she'd felt before.

*That wasn't wind.*

"I just felt the baby move."

"What?" He pressed harder into her abdomen. "I think I felt it. You sure it wasn't wind?"

"I'm sure." She grinned at him and put her hand over his. For a moment, all the worry she had whether or not this would work between them, flew from her mind, and she felt every confidence they would have a future together. All three of them.

"Do I read anything into this. You know... like what we were just doing?" Max suddenly looked very serious, and a little guilty and embarrassed.

Zoe laughed. "I don't think so. But hey... happy Mom, happy baby, right?"

He cupped his hands around her face and kissed her. "I'm so happy we're having a baby."

"Me, too." Her skin prickled from the serious tone in his voice.

"And Zoe…" He brushed his hand down her cheek and she shivered. "I love you."

Warmth flooded through her. "I love you, too."

Zoe leaned forward and kissed him, savoring the moment they shared together. "How about that massage then?"

He chuckled. "Bossy. Come on, I'll have you melting from the touch of my hands in no time."

Zoe quite liked the sound of that. She slipped down from the table and said, "Happy Mom, happy baby."

He tugged her hand, pulling her toward the bedroom. She followed him, happily, glad he wasn't just taking time for her, but also for their unborn baby.

# CHAPTER 2

MONDAY 2ND DECEMBER

Max slipped out of bed without waking Zoe. It was hard to leave her there without taking time to simply embrace her, and snuggle with her before starting his workday. Then again, it wouldn't have stopped at only a cuddle. Things were at a spicy hot level between them, and he was loving the change in his life. He dressed in his usual style of work clothes for the farm —jeans, shirt with the sleeves rolled up, thick woolen socks. His work boots by the backdoor ready for him when he left to start the day.

He needed to go to the far section of the property to check the water levels in the troughs for the cattle. It was summer and it was hot, so he didn't want to risk losing stock from a lack of water. The water reserves were low, but not to the point where they wouldn't make it through to winter without having to buy water in.

He glanced over his shoulder as he walked to the door. Zoe hadn't stirred. She wore long cotton pants with a paisley design, and a singlet top. The sheets were kicked off as the night hadn't cooled to warrant the extra layers. She slept stretched out, slightly on one side, hair messy from sleep, a peaceful expression on her face, and a hand on her belly. What he enjoyed seeing was the little bump of life that was silently growing inside of her. They might not have planned this pregnancy or followed the traditional relationship steps—dating, getting to know each other, trailing living together, then marriage—before starting a family, but he was glad they'd jumped ahead.

Zoe moved.

Max quickly stepped out of the room, leaving her to sleep. He had to get up but she didn't. He felt like he was doing his bit by letting her rest.

In the kitchen, he took out a bowl, filled it with some cereal, then poured cold full cream milk over it. He flicked the kettle on to boil and sat at the table to eat.

Max couldn't believe that Zoe, who was so much younger than he was, could get under his skin like she did. How she'd somehow gotten him to open his heart again after his failed marriage. He never thought he'd have a woman living with him again, let alone one who was carrying their child.

His life had changed so much since the Adelaide Show in September, then again when Zoe had braved driving to his farm in October to tell him she was pregnant. He remembered that day well. How this little city car, totally not built for the rough dirt roads out here, had come bumping along the driveway to his farm. Then seeing her get out, looking hot and sexy, it was a sight to behold. He'd thought he would never see her again, let alone what she was about to tell him. On that day she'd made him a happy man with her news.

Knowing he was going to be a father in a few months kept him working hard on the farm. He wanted things to get into shape before the little bundle arrived, and to get some money flowing. He also needed to tick off the small jobs which had been mounting up. He planned to be a hands-on dad, as much as the farm would let him be, and he wanted to be there for Zoe. She'd risked so much by moving in with him, he felt like it was the least he could do. He wanted her to feel like this was her home too.

It had been only a few weeks since she'd made the move, and he couldn't believe how easily she took such a significant change in her life. Especially when he was still to have the internet upgraded, so she could work more easily and efficiently online. And she was making do with the furniture he had in the place. There was so much that needed to be done to accommodate Zoe, and also for when the baby arrived. He didn't want her to lift a finger, but then again, he couldn't exactly get things done because of his work-load on the farm.

What he had decided was to sell a load of beef cattle. They were looking strong and ready. That was going to be his Christmas gift to Zoe. The money from selling the truckload of cattle could go toward preparing the baby's room and making changes in the house so she could feel at home. He just needed to give the cattle another week, maybe two, so they put on a bit more condition, and he could get a better price at market. Ordinarily, he would've kept them longer, watched the market prices, and avoid selling around Christmas when things were a bit quiet and prices were usually low. Max had decided it was far more important he got some money together, so Zoe could start decorating. He hoped it would also help to give her a purpose during the day. He was worried about how much time she was spending alone. It reminded him, he was going to get his mom to drop in and visit a little more often. She was, of course, super excited with the news, and it was because of her pushing that he was now selling part of his herd.

"Morning." Zoe looked half asleep as she walked into the kitchen, bare feet, her pajama top was pulled tight emphasizing her growing breasts, and her baby bump. He had to admit he quite enjoyed seeing her blossoming. It made him want her more. He felt himself beginning to respond simply from seeing her approach.

"Morning."

"What are you doing today?" she asked.

"Going out to check the water."

"Can I go with you?" asked Zoe. She plonked herself on the chair opposite him, rubbing the sleep from her eyes.

Max bit his tongue. He wanted Zoe to go with him, she had been out with him a few times, but there was also this overprotective part of him that wanted her to stay in the house. It was safe there. Out on the farm there was so many risks.

"I'll just sit in the ute," said Zoe.

Max looked at her. He couldn't resist the puppy dog expression she put on for his benefit. "As long as you're careful."

"Of course, I will be."

"I don't want anything to happen to you, or the baby."

She rolled her eyes dramatically. "It won't. Besides... is your farm like super dangerous or something?"

"No, it's just a normal farm and well, things can go wrong, and accidents happen. There's big machinery and animals after all."

"Then stop worrying."

"I don't think I can," he admitted.

"I'll go get dressed. Don't you leave without me."

"Wouldn't dream of it." He watched her get up, unsure how she'd managed to know what he was partly considering. It was rude of him to leave her behind, but he had considered going quickly right now. He would've done it under the pretense of keeping her safe and sound at home.

"Yeah, you would." Zoe turned back to face him. She pointed her finger and the glare on her face sent a shiver of pleasure down his spine. She had no fear of standing up to him and letting him know her mind.

He loved it.

Secretly.

"If I'm to live here with you, and this is our life together, and our family, don't you go anywhere until I come back."

"Make sure you hurry then."

"Stay," she said, her voice firm as if talking to a dog.

"I think you're learning a lot about farm life already."

She'd obviously heard him talking to his Blue Healer dog, Bluey. It amused him hearing her tone. *She was adjusting well to farm life.* At least he hoped so.

"And I want to learn more by coming with you. So, wait for me." She turned and left, not letting him have the final say, something else which he was used to doing with women. He wasn't sure what it was about her, if it were her youth, how blunt she was or her sass, maybe all of the above, but he found it incredibly attractive.

While he waited, he finished his breakfast, made a flask of tea to take with them, and put some food in the

Esky—banana muffins his mom had made and dropped in the other day, along with some strawberries. Zoe had taken over the cooking, which he was delighted with initially, until finding out that she wasn't at all the best cook. He didn't have time, and he didn't bake, so he'd been relieved when his mom had stopped by the other day with muffins. They'd been surviving on meat and three vegetables, and he often missed lunch. He had a sudden thought that he hoped Zoe wasn't skipping meals. She was pregnant and needed to keep up her strength.

"Ready?" Zoe asked as she came back into the kitchen. She was dressed in a skirt, top, and sandals on her feet.

"Ummm… you're going like that?"

"What's wrong with what I'm wearing?"

"I must say you look totally hot, but you do know that we're going to do farm work and not heading into Burra on a social visit."

"I can't fit into my jeans."

It took Max a moment to realize why. "Sounds like you need to go shopping for new clothes to accommodate this growing baby." He walked up to her and put his hand on her belly. He could feel the firm bump.

This was real.

His life was going to change so much in a few months.

"There's nowhere to shop for maternity clothes in Burra."

Max could believe that. "I'm sure my mom and sister will take you to Adelaide for a shopping trip."

She sighed. "You're not going to let me out to help you?"

"Not wearing that?"

"It's just checking the water. That doesn't sound at all dangerous."

"Yeah, but you know I'm wearing jeans to protect my legs. There are poisonous snakes around here." He expected the mention of snakes to put her off. Instead, her expression darkened with determination.

"You'll need to come up with a better reason than that."

Max could feel himself getting a little hot under the collar. *Couldn't she see that he wanted to keep her and the baby safe?*

"Harrumph." She stalked toward the door. "I'll meet you in the ute."

He stared at her, partly aroused from her defiance toward him and partly in frustration that she could be so stubborn about this. He shook his head, trying to work out how to convince her to stay behind. He had to admit he thought the suggestion of going shopping would've side-tracked her away from wanting to go with him.

"Maaax." The shrill tone of Zoe's voice set his pulse racing and he rushed to the back door.

"What?" He pushed on the screen door and froze. *Fuck.*

"Don't move," he suggested, not believing what he was seeing in front of him.

"Wasn't thinking of moving an inch."

Zoe stood frozen on the concrete footpath that led to the back fence which marked the boundary of the farm homestead. A five-foot-long brown snake was slithering across the path, moving from one side of the dying lawn to the other.

"He'll be out of your way in a minute," he spoke softly, trying to keep calm.

"What, you're not going to do anything?"

"Not with you standing there."

"I won't faint or anything."

Max had to admit, Zoe didn't look at all frightened at the sight of the rather healthy snake slithering on the ground less than three feet away from her. He'd handled more than his fair share of snakes growing up, and living on a farm he'd killed plenty too, without incident. But with her standing so close, the last thing he wanted was to disturb the snake and it flick around and bite her.

"Good. Don't go fainting." He spied an old broom by the back door and went over slowly and picked it up. This snake had made a big mistake coming into his backyard. He had his own family to protect.

The tail of the snake finally slid over the path, and as it kept on its way over the dying grass, Max stepped confidently over to it. Lowering the broomstick, he tried to encourage the snake to wrap around it. He wasn't sure if it was going to work. The snake was long, and heavy, but it was the best approach he had right now. He wasn't about to kill it in front of Zoe. She didn't need such a harsh introduction to farm life and especially not while she was pregnant.

"You going to kill it or what?"

He glanced over his shoulder at her. "Not while you're here."

She huffed loudly. "Aren't they territorial?"

Max wasn't sure how she knew so much about snakes. "True. I'll relocate it."

"Don't you need a bag or something to put it in?"

"Shhh... let me concentrate."

Max inhaled slowly, trying to reduce his pulse, and keep himself calm. Zoe was obvious not rattled by this encounter. At all. He lowered the wooden broomstick a little further, coaxing the snake over it, then he lifted, moving it toward the fence. Luckily the snake didn't protest, and with patience, he got it to slither through a small hole at the bottom of the corrugated iron fence.

He exhaled with relief as it went on its way. If he did have a bag he'd have put it inside, but then again it was a huge snake and he didn't necessarily like his chances of successfully doing that. Hopefully, the snake was just passing through. Max hit the broom on the fence, making a hell of a noise, hoping to let it know that this wasn't a peaceful place for it to decide to call home.

"You think that will convince it to move on?"

"How do you know so much about snakes?"

"Year Ten project in Science." Her voice was entirely matter-of-fact.

He didn't think a year ten project in science would be enough to deal with seeing a brown snake live, they were one of the most dangerous snakes in Australia.

Max strode back to her, perplexed at how calm she was. "Are you all right?" He rested his hand on her bare arm, her skin smooth and hot, and a delight to touch. He shivered. He didn't know what he'd do if anything happened to her or the baby.

"Of course, I am. I only watched a snake do what's natural. It wasn't like it was about to attack me or anything."

He was speechless. Zoe might be a city girl, but she was undoubtedly behaving like a country girl.

"Come on, don't you have water to check?"

"Now, hang on…" Max rushed to catch up with her. "This is why you need to stay here."

"Bloody hell, Max." Zoe spun around her eyes blazing with fortitude. "You want me to stay here to avoid snakes? Well, guess what, there was a snake in the house yard, and I was just fine. I don't see how it's any safer for me here than going out with you to check the water."

Max's eyes widened. He was about to tell her to calm down but managed to stop the words from slipping out. The last thing he wanted to do was to fuel her emotion.

Zoe crossed her arms over her chest and raised an eyebrow at him.

He knew he'd lost the argument. *Too damn easily.*

"Come on then." He stepped in front of her and opened the gate. "After you."

"That's more like it." She smiled at him as she walked past.

He shook his head and managed to grin.

He might just be the luckiest man to have found Zoe, and to have her in his life.

*Don't screw it up.*

# CHAPTER 3

The ute bumped along the fence of the boundary line between Greenfields and the next farm owned by the McLaughlin's. The flat land stretched out in all directions, dry and brown, yet there was a fertile vibe with the hint of green, native trees and bushes, and the cattle casually grazing, ignoring them as they rattled past. In the distance, the Flinders Ranges added a majestic landmark with their mountainous height. The sun's rays felt hot despite it only being mid-morning. Zoe didn't mind the heat so much, though it felt more intense, whether that was because she was further north or because she was pregnant, she didn't know. Maybe it was a mixture of both.

Zoe didn't mind the rough ride in the passenger seat. She didn't wear a seat belt, and she slid around, so she had to grab at the door handle a few times. The window was down, to let in the breeze since the air conditioning didn't work. Zoe had never felt so alive and it beat sitting at home. She enjoyed looking at the landscape of her new home. A shudder slid down her spine. *Could she call this her new home?* A flutter in her belly made her think that perhaps the baby could.

There were a few quick jobs she could've done—legal research she was employed to do working from home for her old firm in Adelaide—but she'd much rather go out and see the farm and spend time with Max. She could imagine that in a few months or so, a ride like this wouldn't be at all comfortable. Besides, the legal work was hard to do with the reduced internet speed, and with the approach of Christmas, the tasks being sent to her had dwindled.

She hadn't told Max this fact though, that she wasn't going to be getting much work for the next few weeks, and she was concerned this might even extend into the new year. Zoe didn't know how else she'd earn an income, and Max had already made it clear that money was tight. All that aside, she did have plenty of time during the day to work at something. Designing the baby's room she knew she could do too, but while she still could she wanted to focus on doing something that would earn money. She wanted to do her bit also for their growing family.

"I'm trying to avoid the bumps," said Max, as he drove the ute.

"Could've fooled me." Zoe felt herself almost lift off the seat of the ute from the impact of hitting a rock.

"Sorry. This is why maybe you should've stayed home."

"Not this again." She turned to look at him, but he kept his attention straight ahead.

Zoe laughed.

"What the hell is so funny?"

"You. And for the record, I'm having the time of my life."

Zoe saw a surprised look on Max's face as he glanced at her.

"Really?"

"Yes, I am. It's certainly more exciting than sitting at a desk all day." She missed the intellectual challenge of her job, but the adventure out there was something more. Like seeing the snake before.

"I guess I should be happy about that."

"Damn right you should, now stop worrying." There was another flutter in her belly, and she put her hand there, wanting to feel the baby again. Would it look more like her or Max? Would it have his dark eyes? Or her blonde hair? Tall like him, or shorter like herself? A bit of her time was spent wondering about what the baby would look like. She couldn't wait to meet the precious bundle.

"Do you think it's a boy or a girl?" she asked.

"Ahhh... it would have to be a boy." He slowed the ute, and turned right, following the edge of the open paddock.

"Because...?" She arched her eyebrow at him. She

supposed it would be typical for a farmer to want a boy with that inheritance thing. Surely, that didn't matter so much these days, though?

"To help me on the farm."

*I was right.* She adjusted her position on the passenger seat, so she was more relaxed, the slower speed more comfortable with less bumping around.

"A girl could help you just as much," Zoe retorted. Whenever she felt like things were going well, there was something, a comment, a niggle from Max that fueled the doubt in her mind.

Max stopped the ute. "We're here. First water trough to check."

"Don't avoid my comment," Zoe demanded. Now they weren't moving, the airflow had diminished and she began to feel the heat of the day.

Max put on the hand brake with an effort. The ute was old, and needed to be upgraded to a newer model a few years ago. "As long as you and the baby are healthy, I don't care if it's a boy or a girl."

"Really?" She wasn't at all expecting that sort of answer from him.

"Yes, really." He reached over and put his hand on her leg. A pulse of desire shot through her skin from his touch. The heat seeped into her, melting away the doubt and the frustration that had been building within her.

"Do you want to find out the gender of the baby?" she asked.

"I dunno…" he scratched his head, "… I think I want it to be a surprise."

"Oh…" She felt a little deflated.

"You don't want it to be a surprise?"

"No, I don't. I want to find out." She was determined to stick to her resolve on this one. To her, it made a lot of practical sense to find out. It determined how she'd decorate the baby's room, and it would mean they would only have to debate over the name for one gender and not two. They could do with fewer arguments.

"I thought it was too soon to find out?"

"I have a doctor's appointment next week at Burra." They had, at least, discussed the fact that closer to the due date Zoe would return to Adelaide so the baby was born in a hospital there, not at Burra where the resources were minimal.

"And you'll find out then?"

"I can. I want to. And, you're coming with me?"

"Of course."

She could tell he'd forgotten about the appointment. It annoyed her. It was easier for him she guessed because his body wasn't rapidly changing. Even she had moments when she forgot she was pregnant.

He sighed heavily. "Let's talk about this later, I need to get these water troughs checked before it gets too hot."

Max got out, not giving Zoe a chance to respond. She clenched her jaw. Maybe this was a conversation to have later, but she didn't like how he avoided it now. There was so much they needed to sort out, and with the approach of Christmas adding to things, she wasn't sure that this was going to happen. She still wasn't sure what they were going to be doing on Christmas Day. She assumed it would be with his family, the threat of a fire meant that Max was reluctant to go far from the farm. Her chest tightened. This would be the first Christmas without her parents, and the last before she became a mom.

Wanting to be part of the farming experience with Max, she got out of the ute. Her feet crunched on dried grass as she walked up to him. A breeze teased her summer skirt around her legs, making her feel cooler. She watched Max check over the water trough. To her, it looked like there was plenty of water. She walked up to the fence, rested her hand on the old wooden post and looked out. This land was all Max's, and it was hard to believe that his family owned so much. Yet, they were hard done by financially. *Would this be what their unborn child would inherit?*

There was so much she still needed to get her head around. The wind lifted, blowing warm air over her, tanging her blonde hair, as she let it take away her thoughts. A sense of peace washed over her. She felt a connection to the earth rise up through her feet, grounding her to the land. There was freedom, space, and life here that she'd never experienced before from living in the city.

Shades of browns with hints of green from salt bushes scattered the landscape. She could hear the cattle off in the distance. The call of a crow was closer, and she spied a cluster of trees nearby assuming it was perched there. A lizard scattered away along the fence line, and another had climbed the next post, looked at her, before deciding to find another spot to bask in the sun. For land that looked like it was dying and was hot and dry, it was full of life.

"All good," said Max.

Zoe turned to face him, not wanting to leave. This was as far as she'd come on the farm with Max. Up until now it had only been very short trips, and she was guessing that was orchestrated out of his concern for her and the baby. *We don't need to be wrapped in cotton wool just yet.*

He smiled at her. The difference they'd had before in the ute was now gone, baked away by the heat of the sun, and then absorbed by the earth they stood on.

"You're hot, you know."

Zoe giggled, tilted her head at him suggestively. "How hot?"

His grin broadened as he strode up to her, wrapped his arms around her from behind and pulled her into his front. "Too hot for me to resist."

She rested her head back on his shoulder as he kissed along her neckline. The sun was hot on her face as she closed her eyes, enjoying Max's lips on her skin, his arms tight around her waist. They might be outside, but it wasn't as if there was any chance of anyone coming along. She relaxed into his embrace, letting him coax the desire from her.

His hands moved over her hips, she could feel the heat of his touch despite her skirt adding a barrier she wished wasn't there. Soft sounds of pleasure came from her, encouraging him to slip his hands over her body, feeling her curves with need.

Gathering up the material of her skirt, her legs bare and exposed to the wind and heat, prickled with anticipation. She leaned back further into him, arching her back, tilting her hips forward, giving him the access he really wanted. His hands brushed up her thigh, leaving a trail of heat that melted into her skin, which caused her pulse to increase. His fingers softly touched the top of her panties, dancing over her mound with such a light touch.

She quivered, a bolt of pleasure moved through her. She could sense his desire for more building with hers, fueling the passion between them.

He traced the pantie line over her thigh, slipped his fingers under the delicate lace, and dipped into her juices. She gasped. Her body convulsed, wanting this to go for longer, she managed to find her resolve, and ride with the building pleasure.

His fingers glided the length of her pussy, between her moist folds, before circling at the top of her slit.

She felt a spike in the pleasure, and reached up behind his head, trying to hold on and ride the wave that was fast, hot, and taking her way too quickly toward her peak. It was as if he could sense her struggle, and he increased his pressure on her intimate folds, building the tension, filling her body with pleasure until it flooded with bliss, and she tipped over into an orgasm with a sharp moan as her body shuddered.

Her mind spun with the desire he'd elicited from her, and she let him take the weight of her body as she slowly absorbed the energy of the orgasm. She could feel his hardness pushing into her, reminding that he was still yet to find a release.

She righted her balance, but before she could turn around to face him, she felt his hands at the top of her panties.

"Ready for more?" His breath was hot on the back of her neck.

She stifled a gasp of anticipation. Her throat tightening with the need for more. All she could do was nod in agreement.

The panties slid down her legs and she stepped out of them. She rested her hands on the wooden fence post to stop herself from losing balance as her mind blurred from the passion burning through her.

His hands firm on her waist, tilted her forward. She could hear him fumbling with his jeans and wished he would hurry up. She wanted him inside of her, giving her the full pleasure her body craved.

The back of her skirt lifted, cotton material moved aside as he positioned his hard cock at the entrance of her pussy. It took the last of her resolve not to tilt her hips back to push him inside of her, and to take a moment to enjoy the pleasure of how her muscles clenched knowing what was about to happen.

He plunged himself into her. She moaned as her muscles parted to receive him, then contract over his cock. Her breath quickened as he pulled out sharply, paused, then returned inside of her, sending a thunderous wave of pleasure through her body. She held tighter on the post, keeping her position, so she could take the full enjoyment of him moving in and out of her. He kept a slow rhythm, while she surrendered easily to the movement. Gradually, he quickened the pace, and she felt the pleasure increasing between them, within her. Her muscles clenched excitedly around his cock as relentlessly plunged in and out of her.

Once more she tipped over into an orgasm, this time with the additional pleasure of him sharing the moment with her. She sighed as her intimate muscles began to settle, and her soul untwined with his back to her own body.

"Aren't you glad I wore a skirt?"

He chuckled. "Things worked out better than I thought it would with you coming along."

"Does that mean I can come with you more often."

He nuzzled, groaning with a tone of mixed emotion. A pang of disappointment hit her gut. Was it expecting too much for him to change a little to accommodate her in his life?

"You know what, I think you can."

She smiled. "See, I can teach an old dog new habits."

"Come here you." He spun her around to face him.

She laughed and squirmed out of his grasp.

"Hey." His arms flayed out trying to grab her, but she kept just out of his reach as she moved toward the ute.

"Come on, don't you have more work to do." She giggled to herself seeing his jeans around his ankles, his cock exposed, and the expression of shock written all over his face.

He bent down, picked up her panties and held them up. "Don't you need these?"

She turned and faced him. A wave of cheekiness took hold of her. She broadened her stance, lifted her skirt, waving it from side to side like a Can-Can dancer, before totally exposing herself to him.

"What do you think?" she called out to him.

"I say, no." He laughed, pulled up his jeans, and slipped her panties into his pocket.

Zoe grinned watching him. This was why they were together, this banter, this sexual tension. She just hoped it was going to be enough of a foundation to start a family together.

\*\*\*

. . .

Zoe had a sense of feeling free as she rested in the ute watching Max check the last water trough. A pleasant buzz vibrated through her body after their cheeky sexual encounter. There was something about having a quickie in nature she mused as he turned and strode back toward her.

"All fine." He got back into the driver's seat of the ute and started the engine. It roared to life.

"Wasted trip?" It had been nearly a twenty-minute drive to get to here from the last stop they'd made.

Max shook his head. "Can't be too careful. The cattle drink a lot of water in a day, so I need to check regularly. Things go wrong out here, and it can mean the loss of lives."

There was a serious shadow to his face. Zoe was starting to get his concern for her and the baby, yet, she wasn't about to give up her independence. She wasn't going to do anything that would be risky.

"You look after me well, Max." She wasn't sure where those words had came from. He did, in his own way, and in a way that sometimes had rubbed her the wrong way. But there was that definite connection between them. After all, as luck had it, or maybe it was Cupid's influence or something, they had created a baby together, even if they hadn't meant to.

He leaned over and kissed her. "I should do more.

But I have plans, Zoe, and I hope you'll not lose patience in the meantime."

Her skin prickled with the tone he spoke in. *Was that what she was doing?* Losing patience. He kissed her again and her thoughts tangled. For now, she only cared that they were together. Details could sort themselves out later. Right?

Max pulled away then stroked her cheek. "Come on, let's get back home. I'm hungry." He put the ute into gear, and with a sharp jerk they skidded.

Zoe muffled a scream, grabbed hold of the armrest to stop herself from crashing into the door.

Max laughed.

She frowned at him, but it was apparent he thought his actions were rather funny. Max continued to grin broadly as he drove back toward home, making a beeline to the nearest road. "Bastard."

Zoe knew damn well he'd done that deliberately. "I thought you were worried about keeping the baby and me safe?" Her heartbeat raced from the scare he'd given her. *Cheeky bastard.*

"What can I say, I like giving you a thrill."

The muscles between her legs clenched tight. Heat flared on her cheeks. He was good at doing just that too. But she wasn't about to tell him.

Max slowed as they approached the gate. "I do, don't I?" He winked at her before getting out and opening the gate.

"You know this is the passenger's job," said Max,

humor thick in his voice as he got back into the ute and edged forward out of the paddock.

"You should've told me... I'll close the gate." Zoe quickly got out as soon as Max stopped the ute. A big gust of wind came along and blew up her skirt.

Max wolf-whistled with a big smirk. "I think you may have converted me to this new dress-wearing style on the farm."

Zoe's felt herself blush as she tried to keep her skirt down. At least it was only Max who was around to see her doing a Marilyn Munroe. She pulled the gate, remembering how to lock it securely based on a previous lesson from Max, then went back to the ute, holding her skirt down.

"Thanks," he relayed as she slipped back into the passenger's seat and closed the door.

"What, for giving you a thrill this time?" She looked at him cheekily.

"That, and for closing the gate. You shut it properly?"

"Go and check." She tilted her chin up in a challenge. "Or, don't you trust me."

"I trust you." To prove it, he put the ute back into gear and turned onto the dirt road.

"Good, so you should." She raised her eyebrow at him, then settled back into the seat, arm on the edge of the open window, enjoying the wind in her hair. This had been a fun outing with Max, and she wasn't just thinking about them having sex. She enjoyed how they interacted. How he didn't shy away from her sharp comments. It almost felt like a date, even though he'd gotten work done.

They were nearly back at the farm when they spotted a car up ahead, coming toward them.

Max slowed. Zoe thought she recognized the steel gray Mazda CX5, but it wasn't until both vehicles stopped side by side when she realized it was his sister Kate, and his mom.

"Hey stranger, about time you came over for dinner," called out his mom, who sat in the passenger seat.

"Just busy."

"We need to sort out Christmas soon, you know?"

"Yeah, I know."

It amused Zoe that Max did what he was told when it came to his mom.

"On your way into town?" asked Kate.

"What makes you say that?" questioned Max.

"Nice outfit, Zoe," said Kate.

Zoe shifted uneasily. She was grateful right now that the material of her skirt was not see-through.

"Oh, that. No, Zoe can't fit into her jeans," answered Max.

"I think a shopping trip to Adelaide is in order," replied Kate, her face lighting with the idea.

"Good idea. We can all go down together, and Zoe? What about if we arrange to have lunch with your parents? We can stay overnight at the Stamford

Grand Hotel, it will be nice to be by the beach for a change."

Zoe swallowed hard. Her heartbeat went a little wild with the prospect of each side of the family meeting. Her parents were good about her move to see if things would work with Max. But still, was she ready for this part in a relationship—the parents meeting each other? She knew Max was sad that his father had passed, and wouldn't get to meet her or his grandchild.

"Sure." She found herself answering despite the opposing thoughts in her mind.

"Great. How about Wednesday? Don't want to leave it too late with Christmas around the corner."

"I will get back to you Mom and sort out Christmas," interjected Max. "And, I can't go on a trip like this right now. I've got things to sort on the farm."

"That's okay, it'll be a girl's trip, just what we need to get to know each other."

Zoe's heart sank knowing that Max wouldn't be coming with her. She'd been with him for nearly a month now, and it was going to be weird to spend the night away from him. That and she didn't really know about spending so much time with Kate and Helen without knowing them.

"I'll check with Mom and Dad, but it should be all right." She couldn't believe she was agreeing to this meetup. Her parents, Robert and Leanne, owned their own business. They sold pharmaceutics and were usually flexible with their hours. Zoe knew they'd jump at the chance to meet Max's mom and sister. They'd already driven to Burra for a lunch with Max just after she'd moved here. To her relief it had gone well. But did she want to sit in the car for a six-hour round trip with Kate and Helen. Plus, overnight with them in a hotel.

Her stomach churned, tightly, and she put her hand on her belly.

"Are you all right dear?" asked Helen, concern thick in her voice. She was in the passenger's seat and partly leaning over Kate.

"Yes, I'm just hungry."

It was a partial lie.

She was hungry, but the pain in her belly was more to do with the prospect of having to spend so much time with Kate and Helen when she didn't know them, and to introduce them to her parents. She knew it was going to happen eventually, it was just that she'd been hoping to orchestrate when that would happen, and not be thrown into it all because she couldn't fit into her jeans anymore. She mused at blaming her jeans for this all happening.

"I better get home then."

"I'll ring you in an hour to make sure we can go Wednesday," said Helen.

Zoe had partly hoped that she might at least delay this until after Christmas. But that was just it. Her parents had been busy, so they hadn't said anything about a Christmas catch up. She figured that they didn't want her traveling in her 'condition.' She managed to stop herself from sighing. One thing was certain, she wasn't going to get out of this one, and it was going to be best to face it all head-on now. Otherwise, it could happen on Christmas Day and she didn't want the added pressure of that. Christmas had a habit of bringing up family emotion, troubles, hurts and problems. Her being unexpectedly pregnant meant that this was a potential minefield.

Her stomach lurched. Zoe moved her hand to her mouth and held her breath, hoping the nauseousness would ease. It did slowly.

"Zoe," said Max. "Don't hurl in my ute."

Of course, that's what Max was more concerned about. She glared at him. Her stomach settling slightly.

"Max, don't talk to her like that," chastised his mom.

"Sorry, it's not what I meant." Max did at least look concerned for her wellbeing.

"Just need some food. It's worse when I haven't eaten, I tend to feel really sick then." She didn't want to tell him that this was nerves about their families meeting, and about spending time with his family. The last thing she wanted was for him to think she didn't want anything to do with his family.

"Go, get her home. You need to get better at looking after Zoe, and my potential grandchild."

Max rolled his eyes, dramatically. "I am, Mom."

"Bye," said Kate.

Max lifted his hand and put his foot from the brake to the accelerator.

"I'll ring in an hour, Zoe," yelled Helen, as the ute pulled away from their car.

"Just as well your mom doesn't know how well you really have been looking after me," said Zoe, trying to lighten the mood.

He smirked. "Just as well."

She rested her head back and closed her eyes. It had been a big morning, and the thought of arranging this meet-up was making her belly a mess of worry. She didn't want to do anything to put Helen off because she wanted to get to know her, and Kate.

*Best get this done and dusted then.*

She planned to ring her parents as soon as she got home. There was no point putting it off any longer, no matter how much she wanted to.

*Home.*

She saw the homestead come into view as Max turned on to the driveway to the farm.

Her belly flipped.

Her hand went over her mouth.

Max slammed on the breaks, and the ute stopped just in time for Zoe to open the door, so she didn't make a mess in his ute.

He leaned over and pulled back her hair. "I'll take the call from Mom later, so you can rest."

Zoe nodded as she wiped her mouth and righted herself back into the ute. She didn't feel any better, though. She wasn't sure where all her energy had gone, and why she suddenly felt so tired. She guessed it was all part of being pregnant. So far, she'd been lucky, and things had gone smoothly with the pregnancy. She'd only suffered from a few bouts of morning sickness. But this was nothing to do with being pregnant.

"I'm sure they will get along fine."

She opened an eye and looked at Max. "How did you know?"

"Hell, my stomach is a mess at the idea, so I just figured yours would be, too. Plus, you haven't been sick much because of the pregnancy. It was an easy conclusion to make."

Sometimes Max surprised the hell out of her.

"Best get it over now and not later."

"I think so."

"And you can't come?" Her eyes pleaded for him to change his mind.

"Sorry. I do need to be home. I have cattle to send away to market, and it can't wait."

Zoe sighed. This was what it was like being on the farm. Max wasn't always able to be by her side. She didn't mind since she was independent, but for this, she reckoned she could do with his support.

*It will be fine*, Zoe kept telling herself. *It* will *be fine.*

If only she believed it.

# CHAPTER 4

WEDNESDAY 4TH DECEMBER

Max lifted Zoe's overnight bag from the bed. "What the hell have you got in here? I thought most of your clothes didn't fit anymore."

"It's not that heavy." She rolled her eyes at him.

"I swear it is." He placed it on the floor for a moment, and scooped her into his arms. "I'm going to miss you tonight."

"Then come." Zoe's eyes pleaded with him to change his mind.

"I'm sorry, I can't."

The truck was coming later that morning to pick up the herd of cattle. Then he had organized his mate, Jim from Burra, to come and install a dish on the roof to help with the internet connection. An early Christmas gift for Zoe. He wanted her to be comfortable, he wanted her to stay, and for all of them to be a family together. It was difficult, because they were still trying to get to know each other. Then the pressure of Christmas, of each other's family wanting to meet, was simply the way it was. They hadn't been careful in the heated moment, and they were both wearing the consequence. For him, this had made him a happy man.

"No?"

He shook his head. It was hard not to blurt out why he was really staying, and to tell her what he was trying to do for her.

"Ring me, any time," he said. "I'm sure our families will get along. Hell, we do, right?"

She put on a brave smile. "Sure."

He sighed. "I look forward to seeing you tomorrow. You and the baby are the best thing in my life." He kissed her slowly, her lips moved with his in a longing that they couldn't address right now.

*Beep. Beep. Beep.*

A car horn sounded outside.

Max pulled away, took his hand in hers. "They're here. Let's not keep them waiting."

"I just need to go to the bathroom once more."

"I'll take your bag to the car then."

"Thanks." She went ahead, while he picked up her bag.

It wasn't really that heavy, he'd been hoping to make her laugh, but she was way too worked up about this trip.

*Maybe I should go with her?*

He pushed on the screen door, slipped on his boots, and then walked out to the car, the bag slung easily over his shoulder. "You ladies ready for some shopping?"

"Absolutely," answered Kate.

"Mornin' Max," called out his mom from the front passenger's seat, waving casually at him as she paused from her knitting.

Kate got out from the driver's seat and opened the boot of the car. Max noticed there was already a reasonable amount of luggage packed in there for an overnight stay.

He raised his eyebrow. "You reckon you'll have enough room for what you want to buy?"

"Of course," Kate huffed.

"Don't you be cheeky now," called out his mom. "You know you should be coming, too."

The tone in his mom's voice caused guilt to cut through his gut.

*He should be.*

But.

There were more important reasons not to.

"Zoe understands," he said slamming closed the boot of the vehicle.

Well, she will be when she sees my surprise for her. Bloody hell, he hoped he could pull it off. Otherwise, he was running being in the doghouse in regard to her, and by the looks of it his mom as well.

Zoe came out from the house, the back-door slamming behind her. The wind caught the navy-blue maxi dress she wore, pushing the material over the bump low in her belly.

He smiled. She looked radiant. Hot. Bloody sexy.

She'd taken time to straighten her hair, and it was styled neatly below her shoulders. For a moment, he thought about canceling what he'd planned for the day to make sure he joined her. It would be fun having a hotel room to themselves. With her ranging hormones adding to the sparks that were already there between them they could have a whole load of adult fun together. But it wasn't possible. He'd already decided he needed to think more long term, for her and for them, and their soon to be born baby.

Max quickly opened the car door for her. "My lady." He winked at her, relieved she smiled back at him. She was undoubtedly putting on a brave face considering how nervous she was when they were in the bedroom packing.

Zoe slid into the SVU, put on her seat belt. He leaned and kissed her goodbye once more. Her salty taste bursting in his mouth in a delight that he hoped would tie him over until tomorrow. She hadn't been on the farm barely a month, and it surprised him how much he didn't want her to leave. It kept his resolve to do whatever he could to make this work between them.

"Don't get up to any mischief, ladies." He closed the

door, enjoying that all three of them were grinning at him.

"Course not," said Zoe. "I am preggers after all."

"Well, since you're not coming, we can do what we want," said Kate as she got back into the driver's seat and started the car.

"Take care." He waved goodbye, watching the vehicle slowly drive away.

This was going to be a long day and night ahead without her.

\*\*\*

Without meaning to, Zoe had fallen asleep in the car for most of the trip to Adelaide. The motion of the vehicle rocking her off to sleep. She woke as Kate slowed at the first set of traffic lights coming into Adelaide on the Port Wakefield highway.

"You should've woken me," she mumbled sitting up and stretching her neck, her muscles stiff from the odd position she'd been sleeping in.

"You need as much rest as you can get," Helen said her knitting needles clicking at a fast pace.

Zoe noticed the fine white yarn she was using. "Are you making something for the baby?"

"A little matinee jacket. It will be winter by the time the baby's born, and it can get cold up at Burra."

It was hard to imagine it being cold, the summer days were hot and sunny.

"It does, especially at night," added Kate. She slowed down at another set of traffic lights. "I hate city driving."

"I can drive if you like," offered Zoe.

"I'll be right."

Zoe bit her tongue. She knew they were trying to be helpful, to let her rest, but it wasn't as if she was sick or not capable. "How about I drive out of the city on the way home, it's easy for me."

"You're not used to driving such a big car."

Her little car was much smaller than Helen's SVU, but she'd driven the ute a little, and she really did feel that she could adapt easily. "Well, the offer's there. I can drive in the city."

"Kind offer," piped up Helen, as she finished a row, turned the growing length of knitted stitches, and started a new one. "Kate doesn't even let me drive." Helen glanced back at Zoe and rolled her eyes.

"I saw that," said Kate, her voice thick with tension. "I saved hard to buy this car."

"You did, and I'm proud of you. Zoe and I would drive it with due care."

Kate ignored them, swearing under her breath as a car cut in front of her. "I'm trying to drive carefully, you know. We do have a pregnant woman on board."

Zoe leaned back, there was no point arguing over this one. It wasn't her car, and it was obvious that Kate was rather attached to it. She understood, it took her a while to save for her own car, but then she'd been on a high salary with her job as a legal secretary. That income was something she did miss, though with no shops at Burra, except for a coffee, gift store and a second-hand shop, the temptation to spend wasn't there like it was when living in the city.

"You're doing a fine job," encouraged Helen.

"You are," added Zoe, realizing that she wasn't the only one on edge.

Zoe looked out, watching the landscape become more populated with houses, and apartment blocks. The traffic became busier. It surprised her how much the noise assaulted her senses. The sound from the vehicles on the road—cars, a few trucks, vans—caused her to feel more closed in, more claustrophobic without being able to see the wide-open spaces that had been her home for the last few weeks. Not being confined to an office for over eight hours a day was also something she didn't miss. Part of her couldn't wait to get back to the farm and feel the freedom of the space. And to see Max, of course.

"I think we might be a little late for lunch," said Kate. "There's too much traffic."

Zoe didn't think there were more cars on the road than normal. "I'll text Mom, to say we will be a little late. She won't mind."

"Thanks," said Kate.

Already things weren't going to plan. Zoe wished

she'd used the excuse of being pregnant to have stayed at home. Her belly roiled, and she rubbed it, as she got out her phone from her small handbag. But then as much as Max might like it, she couldn't walk around the house naked, she needed maternity clothes.

Based on her knowledge of the streets of Adelaide, Zoe texted her mom saying they were going to be about half an hour late.

*That should give us plenty of time to check-in to the Stamford Grand Hotel, freshen up and get ready for lunch.*

The arrangement was to meet in the restaurant of the hotel, which Zoe was relieved, as it took the pressure off now that they were going to be late. Her cell vibrated, and she glanced down to see a message from her mom, who was fine that lunch was going to be delayed. They were already at the restaurant, but were happy to wait.

Zoe guessed her parents might be as nervous as she was to be meeting Max's immediate family. Even though they were obviously over the moon to be able to have lunch with Helen and Kate, and a little disappointed that Max wasn't coming. She wasn't sure why the cattle needed to be sold right now, but since she didn't know enough about farming, she hadn't argue the point.

It felt like she was under the microscope, that both sides of the family were watching her closely to see if things would work out between Max and her.

*Did he feel this pressure too?* She figured he may well, based on his comment when she was sick on Monday.

*Should I talk to him about this?* She sort of didn't want to. With his sharp retorts, and cheeky deflections, she wasn't sure a deep and meaningful conversation was the way to go with him. It was more like a heated argument was more his style. And hers. Since their relationship was built on a lustful attraction, she didn't feel comfortable talking about her feelings with him.

*I'll have to be*, she thought.

Her determination wavering.

Though trusting her feelings when pregnant was something she wasn't so sure was a good idea. This really wasn't the ideal situation to start a relationship.

Yet, here she was. Trying.

*First, I need to get through lunch and a shopping trip.*

This was one shopping trip she wasn't at all looking forward to.

# CHAPTER 5

Max crossed his fingers as he watched the semi-trailer take his cattle away from sale. They would be sold tomorrow. He was banking on a good price, so he could provide for Zoe and their baby. It was always at this point when doubt would slice away at him, and he would begin to question if he should've waited until the new year. But then if he had, it would be much closer to when the baby was born, and he wanted Zoe to have the chance to do her own styling to not just the baby's room, but also to the house. It now was her home too.

*No point thinking about it now.*

Max kicked the stones on the ground, sending them flinging in all directions. He made his way back to his ute. Bluey sat on the back, panting from the workout of loading the cattle.

"Reckon she'll like what I have planned?" He patted

Bluey behind his ear. The dog leaned in harder to his palm, enjoying the scratch. Max wished he was like Bluey without a care in the world.

*Maybe I should've talked this over with her.*

It wasn't his style. He'd been alone for so long now. Zoe had turned his life upside down, and not just with the news of being pregnant. He wanted to do right by them both. This was the only way he knew how, by giving her a gift of money so she could do some renovations and feel at home.

*Would this be what she wanted?* He shrugged, as he got into the ute. He didn't really know. They had been doing what new couples did early in a relationship, sex and lots of it.

He started the engine, then drove back the short distance to the house, where Jim was working on the roof to attach the satellite dish. Max figured the boosted internet might help Zoe connect with her city life, and not feel so isolated. It was different for him, life in the country, on a farm, was all he knew. He was sure about one thing though, he couldn't move to the city. For his family, he'd give it a go, but that lifestyle wasn't for him. It was bad enough each year when he went to the Royal Show in Adelaide. He was a country boy through and through.

He slowed as he approached the old homestead.

"Nearly finished?" he called out from the open window of his ute at Jim, who was on the roof.

Jim nodded and gave him the thumbs up.

At least he should have two surprises ready for Zoe when she came home. He wanted her to like them, and realize that's the real reason he stayed behind. Small sacrifices for a bigger picture. He hoped his plan would please her.

\*\*\*

"Look how much you've changed already," exclaimed her mom. Zoe walked into the restaurant area at the Stamford Grand Hotel. They had finally arrived, and Zoe had gone straight to see her parents, leaving Kate and Helen to check-in. They assured her it would be fine.

"Mom." Emotion rose up inside of her and her eyes filled with tears as she embraced her mom. She'd missed her. Her dad stood from the table and came over. She let go of her mom to hug her dad.

"Dad, how are you?"

"How's my favorite daughter." He hugged her tightly, then sat back down at the table by the window which gave a view of Glenelg beach.

Zoe grinned, she was their only child, and her dad's comment was an ongoing joke he had with her.

Her mom patted her belly. "How's my little grandie going?"

"Mom." She pushed her mom's hand away, and

grinned. It was good to be with her parents again. Another wave of emotion washed over her. Zoe dabbed the corner of her eye with her finger.

"Oh, darling, it's just the hormones. Being pregnant does that." Her mom hugged her again.

"Does it?" Zoe couldn't resist the sarcasm.

"It's not for much longer." Her mom handed her a handkerchief.

"It will be the longest six months of my life, I just know it." Zoe pressed the material at the corners of her eyes, hoping she hadn't smudged her makeup. It felt like ages since she'd taken the time to style her hair and to put on makeup. It was too easy to be casual on the farm, and Max certainly wasn't complaining about her natural style.

Leanne smiled sympathetically at her daughter. "Enjoy it. It's a special time."

Zoe nodded, not trusting herself to talk without managing to cry. *Is this what was ahead of her for the next six months?* If so, she was going to be glad to hide away on the farm.

"Here, take a seat, and tell me what's been going on." Her mom pulled out the chair at the head of the table for Zoe to sit, then sat to her left, next to her dad, leaving the other side free for Kate and Helen once they'd checked in.

"Not a lot has been happening." Her makeup more than likely smudged, she was wearing a dress that was something she would consider casual, and definitely not upmarket enough for here at this restaurant, Zoe felt uncomfortable and out of place. It was amusing at first that her jeans no longer fitted, but now, the realization of what that meant, and how her body was changing was a little scary.

"What you need is a hobby," said Leanne. "Something that isn't on your computer."

"I don't need a hobby, Mom," answered Zoe, unsure why on earth her mom would suggest something like that. She'd always been a workaholic, and never had time for hobbies. There were the occasional times she spent going to the gym, burning off the frustration of a day's work in the legal world, but there was no gym on the farm, or in Burra come to think of it. While some women went off to the gym when pregnant, she wasn't one of them.

"It will help to keep your mind occupied."

"I think my mind's occupied enough," she mused. There was the getting used to living with Max, being pregnant, getting to know his family and adjusting to farm life. There was more than enough to keep her thinking. Then there was the occasional work she was doing remotely for the firm she used to work for, and the worry of how long that would last.

"My point exactly. You're dealing with so much... a hobby will help take your mind off of it all."

Zoe wasn't sure she needed anything else to consider in her life right now.

"Think about it, Zoe. You don't have to." Her mom

picked up the bottle of water on the table and poured Zoe a glass. "It's just a suggestion."

Zoe knew damn well her mother never made a 'suggestion.' It was more like, this is what you should do, and I'll keep on about it until you do.

"I just can't imagine myself making a quilt, Mom. Can you?" Zoe was rather pleased with her response. *That should shut her up.*

"No, I can't either. So, maybe don't try that as a hobby right." Her mom's eyebrows arched, and Zoe felt herself squirming as if she hadn't really shut her mom up at all.

*Will I do this to my child?* She decided she definitely wasn't going to do the 'guilt trip' on them, no matter what.

"Now, why isn't that man of yours down here with you?" asked her dad. He filled the glasses on the table with water and looked up for an answer.

"Like I said, he's busy with cattle. Had to get it done before Christmas." She wished he was here with her. But then a ripple of something went through her and her tears dried, and she felt a renewed strength take hold. This was more like her. Strong. Independent. Fearless.

"Couldn't wait?"

"No." She hoped that Max doing this job now would free him up for Christmas. Then they could spend the time to really get to know each other.

"You know, Zoe, if it's not working out with him

you can come back here. We will support you," said Leanne, her forehead wrinkled with genuine concern.

Her mom's comment made her uneasy. She loved Max. She wanted it to work out. This was part of being in a relationship with a farmer, and she was independent. Yet, the emotion burned through her. Here she was about to juggle both sides of the family meeting up without him, and she couldn't help but resent him a little.

"I'd be happy for you to come back, too," spoke her dad.

"It's good to know you're both here for me." She wasn't about to open up and tell them her doubts or say that everything was fine. Things weren't bad. They weren't even at a point where she thought about returning to Adelaide because she couldn't tolerate living on a farm. But would she continue to meet the challenges of the isolation while pregnant, and not knowing many people where she was now living. For now, the big question was whether or not it would stay like that.

"Consider it an option, a sort of safety net," said her mom.

"Thanks." Zoe was sure her mom would be excited to see her grandchild as much as possible. And both her parents were doing what they considered was their duty of looking out for her.

"You must be Leanne and Robert," Helen said as she walked up to the table. She smiled broadly and put out her hand to her mom. She'd changed into a light summer dress, gray hair brushed, and Kate followed behind, wearing jeans and a loose summery transparent shirt.

"Oh, we're practically family, a hug is in order." Leanne got up and embraced Helen warmly.

"And you must be Kate." Leanne gave an equally welcoming hug to Kate, who looked a little uncomfortable with the familiarity on display.

"Good to meet you both." Robert held out his hand, but Helen taking the cue from Leanne, stepped around the table and hugged him. Zoe tried not to cringe, she'd never hugged Helen or Kate, they just didn't come across as the type to greet each other like that, which was fine with her.

"We're family, right?" Helen grinned. "So glad to finally meet you both."

"What about some bubbles?" asked Leanne.

"Great idea," said Kate. "Settle my nerves after driving in the city."

"That bad?" asked Leanne.

"Yep."

"Well, Robert can drop us off in the city and we can go shopping, and when we're ready he'll come pick us up."

"I will?"

Leanne patted her husband on the arm. "Yes, you will, and we will all be so grateful."

Robert rolled his eyes. "I need Max here, I'm feeling outnumbered."

"That reminds me..." started Leanne.

Zoe felt a flip in her belly, one that was fully of foreboding. *What the hell was her mom about to say?*

"I just don't know how to say this, so I'll just say it as it is." She took a deep breath. "We are concerned that Max isn't there for Zoe."

Her father nodded in agreement.

Zoe's eyes widened, a sinking feeling rose from inside, and she looked between Helen and Leanne, the two women previously so friendly, now eying each other off as if they were about to charge each other.

"Where is a waiter?" asked Zoe, turning around while trying to diffuse the situation.

The waiter caught her eye and came over.

Zoe could feel the tension increasing at the table.

"Some bubbles, please." She couldn't drink alcohol, but she hoped that the champagne might change the vibe that was now consuming the table.

"My son is looking after Zoe just fine." Helen's words clipped sharply in the air.

"Where is he then?" shot back Leanne.

*Bloody hell, Mom, don't hold back.* Zoe took a deep breath. They were going to need more than bubbles right now to settle this situation.

"Working on the farm. Making sure there's a future for his child."

"Surely, he could have taken one day off. Come down and meet us. All of us. Together. You know, this is just as important for his future, too."

*Oh God*. Zoe's mind went into overdrive trying to come up with a way to stop this argument.

"Sometimes that is just not possible," Helen replied defensively.

"And when is it then? Will he manage to be there for the birth? Or will farm work get in the way again? I don't like my daughter being unsupported."

"We are supporting her," snapped Helen. A dark expression shadowed her usually carefree face.

"How? Zoe never mentions that she's seen you when we talk over the phone."

"We're here now, meeting you, and we're going shopping. I want to give her and Max space, they have a lot of adjustments to make."

"It's all right, Mom," interrupted Zoe, finally finding her voice. An idea sparked in her mind. "You can meet us all over Christmas. Come to the farm for a few days. Then you can see Max, and if he's really supporting me or not."

"Harrumph." Her mom sat back on the chair. "I think we might just take you up on the offer and see for ourselves. I did think that he's a nice enough boy, but seeing my daughter here, without him, looking tired and emotional, I now have my doubts."

"I don't look that bad, do I, Mom?" Zoe hoped her mom was putting on the drama. She was feeling tired, but it had more to do with this argument, and that she'd just invited her parents to Greenfields for Christmas without consulting Max than anything else.

*I hope he won't mind.*

"Sorry, Zoe, I'm just worried for you. You're on the farm so far away from medical help. Maybe you should come back here sooner before the baby is born. Better to be safe than sorry."

"Mom, I think *you* need to have a hobby."

"Zoe, please don't speak to me like that."

"Let's just have lunch, get to know each other, not lay any unnecessary blame."

Helen sighed heavily. "I think—"

Zoe held up her hand. "I don't need this kind of stress, and right now you are all stressing me out."

"Sorry, Zoe," said her mom quickly. "But—"

"No." Zoe cut her mom off from saying any more. "This is what will happen now. We will have lunch, talk politely, and I suggest we plan the Christmas meal together. You don't want me to cook it after all, which has nothing to do with me being pregnant and everything to do with my lousy cooking. You've both accepted this unexpected pregnancy, and now we have to find ways to get along with each other's differences." Zoe inhaled to try and catch her breath.

The baby flipped in her belly. *Glad you agree with me.*

She glared between Helen and her mom, both women clenched their jaws, as if really stopping themselves from saying what they wanted to.

"Do you agree or not? If not, then I'm leaving." It was a snap decision, but she meant it wholeheartedly.

An uncomfortable silence settled between the

women.

"Fine then." Zoe went to stand.

"Don't go," said her mom, reaching out and grabbing her hand. "I'll agree."

Zoe turned to Helen, waiting for an answer. "You both have to agree. Otherwise, I'm leaving."

"Fine! I agree, too."

Zoe sat back down. "Good. And don't forget, at any time today, if there are comments flying I *will* leave."

Tension built through the back of her shoulders, and her lower back. The stress caused an uneasy feeling in her stomach. She found that if she didn't eat something at regular intervals, she felt queasy. "Let's order, too. I'm hungry." She picked up the menu.

Her mom and Helen still glared at each other, but they kept silent as they followed Zoe's lead. Kate sat there uncomfortable, along with her dad, both seemingly too scared to say anything.

"Kate, you're more than welcome to join us for Christmas, too," said Zoe. She knew Kate was single, but she didn't want her to think she wasn't welcomed.

"Thanks," said Kate politely.

"I would imagine, with the wonderful cooks on this table…" Zoe was referring to Helen and Leanne, "… that you probably won't need me to bring anything."

Kate grinned at her comment. Slowly, the tension began to ease.

"Helen, would you like to cook the turkey roast? And Mom, you can be in charge of the dessert. Maybe an ice cream version of Christmas pudding?"

"I'd rather desert, you know," said Helen quietly.

Zoe was about to speak when her mom quickly interrupted. "And I'd rather cook the mains. Want to swap?"

"Yes. And you don't have to cook a traditional turkey roast if you don't want to," suggested Helen with a smile.

"I wouldn't know what to cook if I didn't roast a turkey," grinned Leanne.

"Neither would I. But I thought I'd mention it, you know, in case you had your own family recipe you wanted to cook."

"Bubbles all round?" asked the waiter as he returned with a bubble of champagne.

"Not for me," said Zoe.

"Or me," said her dad.

Zoe caught his eye and he winked.

She smiled inwardly.

Things might work out after all, with the family lunch and a shopping trip.

# CHAPTER 6

"It great," said her mom. "Look at your cute bump. You got to show it off now."

Zoe wasn't sure. She was tired and beginning to feel a little unwell. This was the third shop that they had been in. Things weren't so tense between Helen and Leanne now, but the strain was still there.

Zoe forced herself to look in the change room mirror. The jeans fitted well enough, but she just wasn't used to the stretchy band at the top to accommodate her growing a baby. The black and white top was tight, and showed off her bump. She felt a little self-conscious noticing how big her breasts were getting.

*No wonder Max can't keep his hands off them.*

The thought helped to improve her mood. It was telling how much she missed him. It was the reassurance she needed right now for herself that she was attracted to him, and being pregnant aside, she did actually want to be with him and building a life together. It seemed her mom thought Max should be doing more. Zoe was starting to think the same, but then Helen had been so defensive. She just didn't know enough about farm life to be able to tell if Max was using this as an excuse not to come with her or not. She hoped he wasn't.

"I dunno, it feels funny on my belly." Zoe flicked the top of the jeans, the stretchy material coming up over her belly button, and not at all where jeans were meant to sit.

"Trust me, you'll grow into it."

Zoe didn't want to think how big her belly was going to get.

"Come on out and show us." Helen's legs were hurting from varicose veins and so she sat in the corridor of the change rooms with Kate keeping her company.

Her mom held open the curtain, suggesting she went out to show them. This had been the routine for the afternoon, and Zoe was starting to tire of it. It did seem that her mom and Helen, even Kate, were having more fun at picking out the clothes than she was. Despite the tension between the older women, they weren't saying anything to put Zoe off.

What Zoe really wanted was to have arranged to meet up with her friends Ellie and Billie, but they told her they knew nothing about buying maternity clothes.

Billie was further north near Port Augusta, doing some shearing, and Ellie was back on her farm in the south-east, and neither of them couldn't make it today. They did, at least, promise to come to the baby shower when she had it.

"Very nice, I like it," said Helen as Zoe stepped out of the change room.

"You do?"

"Yes. You can wear it out on the farm with Max," said Kate.

"If he lets me go with him."

"Why wouldn't he?"

"I think he's worried something will happen to me."

Kate rolled his eyes and looked at her mom. "We better talk to him."

"Yes, we will do just that. Don't worry, if he ever causes you to get upset come to me, and I'll give him a good telling off. He needs it often, you know."

Zoe couldn't help smiling. "I know."

She glanced at her mom and noticed a change in her expression. *Maybe she was coming back around toward Max.*

"I'll buy this one for you," said Helen.

"No, it's fine," Zoe said quickly. Money was tight, but it was tighter for Helen. Zoe had been saving for a deposit on a house, but since that wasn't going to happen, and now only doing a little work from home for her old firm, she was spending her savings.

"I insist."

Zoe sensed how much joy this was giving Helen. So, she decided to let this one go. "Just this once."

"Pfft." Helen grinned. She elbowed Kate. "Show her the other dress you found."

Zoe managed to stop herself from rolling her eyes. This had also been part of the routine this afternoon. All three of them were finding maternity clothes for her to wear. Between them they had already picked out an outfit she could wear for the baby shower they were now planning for late March next year. There was a lovely dress for when she came home from hospital with the baby. They also had her get some clothes suited for breastfeeding. Zoe's mind spun from how much she was learning about having a baby, and it was all through buying clothes. She was struggling to keep up with the information overload.

Kate held up a dress. It was a white, baby doll style, with open red rose pattern on it. Zoe had to admit it looked beautiful. Something she would wear if she was living in the city, but not the farm.

"I love it. But don't you think it's a bit fancy?"

"For Christmas? No way. We dress up for the day," said Kate.

"Okay." Zoe took the dress, but she was still hesitating. She had planned to be conservative with spending today, but these women weren't helping. At all.

"Try it on and see," suggested Helen.

Zoe slipped back into the change room, and took off the jeans and top, slipping the dress on over her head. She twirled around, looking at herself in the mirror. This was more like the clothes she was used to wearing. She loved it.

"Let's see," called out her mom.

She was relieved how well her mom was getting along with Helen and Kate now, and vice versa. She didn't like being told what to do. But wearing this dress, somehow made her feel better, like she could bring a part of her city self to the farm and it be all right to do so. Zoe stepped out to show them.

"You have to get it," said Helen straight away.

"You do," stated her mom.

"Yep," Kate reassured.

"I'll get it, but I'm buying this one myself," said Zoe firmly. She braced herself for an argument and wasn't surprised when she got one.

"No. I insist," said Helen.

Suddenly, Zoe felt unsteady on her feet.

She felt the world sway to the left, then to the right.

The voices from Helen and Leanne arguing sounded distant as she blinked a few times.

"Are you okay?" Kate moved toward her.

Zoe wasn't feeling well, and she didn't know why. She was about to lie and say she was fine, hoping that this sensation would go away, but then the room spun fast and she was falling.

\*\*\*

. . .

"Zoe, thank goodness," her mom spoke softly nearby.

Zoe eyes fluttered open. She wasn't sure why she was on the floor in the change rooms. The fluorescent lights above hurt her eyes, and she moved her arm to cover her face. There was something soft under her head.

"An ambulance is on its way," said Kate.

"What?" Zoe tried to sit up. "I don't need an ambulance."

"You fainted. You're having a ride in the ambulance whether you like it or not," said her mom firmly.

"You're overreacting, Mom," Zoe mumbled.

The floor was uncomfortable, and she moved to sit up.

"You should stay lying down," said Leanne.

"I'm fine."

It was a lie.

The room swayed.

Zoe was determined to stay sitting up, at least. She breathed in deeply in an attempt to settle the response. She didn't want a fuss made over her.

"I think it's best you go to the hospital. Get a doctor to check on you and baby," said Helen.

"I agree," said Leanne.

Zoe wasn't about to go to the hospital. There was nothing wrong. All she wanted to do was to go back to the hotel. She was certain she'd feel better after a few hours rest, and some room service.

"Did you want something to drink?" asked Kate, handing her a bottle of water.

Zoe nodded, taking the bottle. She took a sip, the liquid cooled and helped to settle the dizziness that was still lingering.

*Maybe I should go to the hospital?*

The thought made her queasy. She'd never been in hospital. She took another deep breath. "I'm feeling a bit better," she lied.

"Good," said an ambulance officer as she came into the change room. "That's what I like to hear."

Zoe looked up at her. "I'm sorry to have bothered you."

"Oh, I don't think that you have at all." The ambulance officer turned around. "Right, few less people here, thanks."

Reluctantly, Helen and Kate shuffled out of the tight space, leaving Zoe with her mom and the ambulance office.

"She's pregnant," said her mom seriously.

"Congratulations." The officer gave a warm smile which helped to make Zoe feel more at ease. "My name is Steph."

"Zoe."

"I'm going to take your blood pressure and temperature. Have you hurt yourself from falling?"

"She was out cold for a few seconds," replied her mom.

*Was I?* That didn't sound good.

She let Steph take her blood pressure, and her smile faded a little.

"High?" asked her mom.

"Low," said Steph. "I'm sorry, miss, but you're going to have a quick trip to the hospital."

"The baby?" She didn't feel any pain in her belly, but she didn't know how she was meant to be feeling.

"That's why we're going to the hospital, to be sure."

Zoe nodded, but her belly flipped with nerves. She put her hand on her stomach, hoping to feel the bubbling sensation that she associated with the baby's movement, but there was nothing.

"I'm sure everything will be fine," reassured her mom.

This baby wasn't planned, but Zoe knew she would be devastated if something went wrong and she lost it.

\*\*\*

The ten-minute trip in the ambulance to the Women's and Children's Hospital felt like it was more like an hour. The emergency section was busy, and Zoe was wheeled into a section in the corner, the curtain was drawn and she was told to wait for the doctor who would soon be here.

Her mom sat on the edge of her bed, holding her hand.

"I better tell Max," said Zoe. "Can you pass my cell?"

"No, you need to rest."

"It's only a phone call." She wanted Max by her side, and the fact that he wasn't, made her irritable.

"I'm sure Helen and Kate will let him know."

*What the hell would they tell him.* A new worry started in her mind. She shifted uncomfortably on the bed. He didn't need to know everything. Maybe it would be better to tell him after she'd seen the doctor.

"Zoe Preston?" A female doctor poked her head through the gap in the curtains.

"Yes," Zoe answered.

"I'm Dr. Khatri."

Zoe smiled weakly, trying to think positive. She hadn't felt any bubbly-like movement, only flutters of nerves. *Had anything bad happened when she fell?*

"Is there any bleeding?"

Zoe shook her head. That was one good sign Steph had told her in the ambulance on the way to the hospital.

"That is a good sign."

A nurse came into the cubicle space, holding ultrasound equipment. "I'm Jean, let's hear your baby's heartbeat."

Jean helped Zoe to move the material of her maxi

dress, so the sensor could be pressed into her abdomen. Zoe held her breath, as a static noise came from the machine.

Then she heard it.

A faint heartbeat.

She smiled.

The baby was fine.

"That's a good sound, isn't it," said Dr. Khatri.

Zoe nodded, feeling her eyes water with tears.

Everything was fine.

There was no need for all of this fussing.

"So, this is what's going to happen. I'm going to check you in—"

"I have to stay?" Zoe interrupted, she had started to get her hopes up about going back to the hotel, ringing Max, and laughing over this incident.

"Your blood pressure is a little low, and you're due for your 12-week scan. So, I'm going to run some tests."

"Oh..." Zoe's shoulders slumped at the news.

The doctor placed her hand on Zoe's arm. "Just think, in a few hours you're going to see the ultrasound of your baby. That will make up for it all."

"I can't wait."

"But Max isn't here." Zoe couldn't hide the emotion in her voice.

"Well, tell him to come," said Dr. Khatri.

"He's nearly three hours away."

"Then he better hurry. I want to get the scans done as soon as possible to be sure everything is on track."

*Bloody hell.* Zoe sighed.

This wasn't at all how the shopping trip was meant to end up.

\*\*\*

Max finished collecting the eggs, placing them carefully in his Akubra hat, before slowly closing the door and locking the hens in for the night. It was late afternoon. Jim had finished installing the satellite and the truck driver had called to tell him the cattle had arrived safely.

Bluey trotted next to him as he walked back to the house, wondering how Zoe was getting on with the shopping trip. A text a few hours ago only told him that they'd arrived in Adelaide and were going to have lunch soon.

"Just you and me tonight, boy," he said, kicking his boots off at the back door, and heading inside, glad to be finally out of the heat of the day. Bluey followed him, his face happy that he could once more get the privileges he'd lost when Zoe had moved in.

*Zoe.* He missed her right now.

Max put the eggs in the fridge, took out a beer, and

was about to head back outside to sit on the veranda and watch the sunset when his cell rang. He put the beer on the table—disappointed to see his mom's name flashing on the screen and not Zoe's—and he answered it.

"Hi, Max."

"Hi, Mom. How's the shopping trip going? Run out of money already?"

"I'm sure it's nothing…"

His heart thundered in his chest while his thoughts went immediately to Zoe.

*What the hell had happened?*

*The baby?*

*Were they all right?*

"Zoe's been taken to the Women's and Children's Hospital."

"What?"

"Kate and I are on our way there. Well, we're going back to the hotel to pick up her overnight bag, then to the hospital."

*Fuck.*

His hands shook.

He near collapsed on the kitchen chair nearest to him.

"Max, you there?"

He pulled himself together. "What happened, Mom?"

"She collapsed when shopping."

"Shit." That couldn't be good.

"Her blood pressure is low. Anyway, doctor's doing tests and keeping her in hospital overnight."

*That didn't sound like nothing.*

"I'm sure it's only a precaution, Max."

"I hope so." He ran his hand through his hair. "I'll come now."

"Good. I was about to tell you that you should."

"I'm on my way."

Max swallowed hard, trying to focus. He should really shower, grab a few things, but all he wanted to do was get to Zoe as quickly as he could. She was a three-hour drive away, and he didn't want to waste one second getting to her.

\*\*\*

Zoe lay back in the uncomfortable hospital bed in a private room. She was lucky to have a room of her own, but she didn't feel lucky. The room was small, there was a private bathroom to her left, a small window to her right, which looked out onto the parklands. It smelled of cleaning fluid and it appeared sterile. This was meant to be her time to rest but doing nothing was driving her crazy. The television didn't work, and she couldn't bring herself to read the out-of-date magazines like her mom, who was on the chair by the bed. Whatever article she was reading it was taking her attention.

Zoe leaned over, grabbed her handbag off the side table, and took out her phone.

The screen was blank.

No messages from Max.

No calls.

She felt like throwing it across the room in frustration.

*Did he not care? Was he simply too busy?* Either way, she wanted him here with her. Now. Since he wasn't, it was too easy to think negatively toward him.

"Your dad will visit later," said her mom looking up from the magazine. "What are you doing with your phone? You're meant to be resting."

"Staring into space isn't resting."

"Being on your phone isn't resting either."

"I'm finding myself a hobby," said Zoe sarcastically.

Her mom put down the magazine. "There's no need to take that tone with me."

Great! It's like I'm a teenager all over again. Zoe realized that if things didn't go well with Max and her, going back to live with her parents would create a whole new set of problems for her to deal with.

Her phone vibrated. A photograph of Max came up on her screen which made Zoe smile. Finally.

"Max..." Tears welled in her eyes.

"Zoe, what happened?"

"Nothing." She didn't even know how this all happened, or what had actually gone wrong.

"Sounds a bit more than that."

Her mom got up from the chair. "I'm going to grab a coffee."

Zoe waited for her mom to leave.

"I want you here," demanded Zoe.

"I'm on my way."

"It's not g-good enough," her voice started to crack.

"Hey, I'll be there soon."

Words caught in Zoe's throat in the lump of emotion.

"I love you, Zoe."

The anger she was experiencing toward him melted. "I love you."

"I'll see you soon. You take care, and look after yourself and baby."

The call ended.

Zoe wiped her eyes and put away her phone. She wasn't sure how long it was going to take for Max to get here, but it was going to be too long.

"Knock, knock." Her mum walked back into the room. "Helen and Kate are here with your bag."

"Thanks." The thought of being able to wear her pajamas was comforting. She wanted to get out of the maxi dress she'd been wearing all day. And the chance to shower using her favorite strawberry soap was overwhelming.

"We also have some of the clothes from today," said Helen.

"Hope you don't mind, but we grabbed a few things off the rack which we reckon will look great on you, after you left in the ambulance. Just because you're in the hospital doesn't mean you don't want to wear something that will make you feel better."

"Thanks." Zoe surprised herself with her response. She didn't mind that they'd picked out some clothes for her. It was as if this incident had made her come a little more to terms with how much she's no longer in control of her life.

"I'll show you. Maybe you might like to wear these now," suggested Kate as she pulled out a dark pink top and charcoal harem-styled pants.

"They look great." Zoe smiled. "I'll put them on now." She got out of the bed carefully and went and changed in the bathroom, glad to be able to freshen up a little, and to move around instead of lying on the bed.

The doctor wasn't sure when the scan would happen, but it would be today sometime.

I might be used to waiting after this baby is born. The thought amused her, as she came out of the bathroom.

"Good choices," said her mom.

Helen and Kate had managed to find an extra chair from somewhere and were sitting on them lined up under the window.

"They're comfy," said Zoe, as she got back on the

bed, and sat crossed-legged. "Plenty of room for growth."

"Max is coming down now," said Helen.

"I know, he rang just before."

"You know initially I was so frustrated he wouldn't come for this trip, but you know, farm work sometimes can't wait. I should know, I was married to a farmer myself for twenty-eight years. I so wish he'd be here… to see his grandchild born."

Kate hugged her mom. "He's here in spirit."

Zoe steeled herself against the emotion that vibrated between them all. Her eyes teared up again, and she used the handkerchief to stop them from falling.

"Yes, I'm sure he is." Helen inhaled, as if pushing away the emotion. "I can't wait for you all to come to the farm for Christmas."

"Yes," said Leanne. Her eyes lit up. "It will be a lot of fun to have Christmas on a farm."

Zoe groaned as if in pain. This was actually going well. Maybe, too well. They were bonding, and she felt as if she was trying to put on the brakes to slow things down.

*Maybe I shouldn't?* Something she momentarily thought might be a good idea with Max too. It wasn't that long ago she'd tried to convince herself to let the details sort themselves out. Hard to do for someone like herself who preferred to be in control.

"Best let them go on this, Zoe," said Kate. "I know there's no stopping my mom when she gets like this."

"I agree," said Robert.

Zoe nodded. She wanted her parents with her for Christmas. It would be timely if they came to her new home. She just hoped Max was going to be all right with what his mom was planning, encouraged whole-heartedly by her mom. She inhaled slowly, hoping to settle the flutter of nerves in her belly. She had been worried that not everyone would get along.

*How wrong was I?*

Instead the opposite was happening. Helen and Leanne were getting on famously, and her dad, as usual, was going along with the flow.

"Now tell us, Zoe. Is it a girl or a boy?" asked her mom. "I need to know what to start buying."

"I guess I'll find out with the scan." She swallowed hard, remembering that Max didn't want to find out. *But I do*. And Max wasn't there.

"Good," said Helen. "I want to know, too. Stuff this waiting for a surprise until the baby is born."

"Mom," interrupted Kate. "This is Zoe and Max's choice." She turned and looked at Zoe. "But as the only aunty to this baby, I would like to know the gender beforehand. I plan to spoil him or her and be the favorite."

"Good luck with that," challenged Helen. "I'm going to be the favorite."

"No, way, I am."

"Don't forget about me," interjected her dad.

This was what Zoe was worried about, but the women were all smiling. "You'll all be baby's favorite."

"But you're right. Zoe, what do you want? Secret or not?" Helen looked at Zoe, waiting for an answer.

"I'd like to find out."

"Great." Leanne smiled. "You can tell us all next week."

"Yeah, but—"

"I can't wait to find out if it's a girl or a boy," said Helen. "I think it might be a girl."

"Oh, I do. too."

"I dunno, I think it's a boy," said Kate.

*When had they all decided on the gender of her baby?*

Hell, she had no idea if it were a boy or a girl. She was still trying to come to terms with being pregnant, and in a relationship, and living hundreds of miles away from the only city she'd ever lived in.

*What was she going to do now?*

*How was she going to handle this potential situation?*

Zoe doubted that her mom or Helen would be able to keep the gender a secret from Max, and he didn't want to find out.

*Did his opinion matter?* She was carrying the baby. And why should she not find out because he didn't want to.

*Was this the crack that would push them apart?*

. . .

85

\*\*\*

Zoe looked at the screen trying to determine if her baby was a girl or a boy. She didn't know how anyone could tell. To her it was a smear of gray tones. A mess. Her mom hovered by her side. A hospital rule meant only one person could be with her.

"Do you want to know the gender?" asked the technician.

Zoe paused.

She did.

But Max didn't.

*He's not here.*

They hadn't really discussed whether or not they would find out. Other than she had said yes, and Max no.

"You don't have to find out," said her mom.

Zoe looked at her. "Really."

"It is your choice. And to be honest, it should be something between you and Max."

"But he's not here."

"I'm sure there are reasons for it."

"The farm."

The technician moved the probe over her belly.

"I want to know."

"You sure?"

Her mom wasn't helping.

"I do. I don't want to wait any longer. Besides, she knows already."

"I do," said the technician. "Ready to find out then?"

"Tell me…"

"It's a girl."

Zoe smiled. *A girl.* "Can I have a photo of the image?"

"Of course, I'll print a few."

"Is everything all right with her." It felt good to say the baby's gender.

The technician's previously poker face broke into a smile. "Your baby is perfect weight and growing well."

That was the best news Zoe had heard all day.

Now, the problem was, how to tell Max she knew the gender of their baby.

# CHAPTER 7

Max hurried into the hospital. Kate had texted him the room number, and after asking at reception for directions, he was about to finally see Zoe.

He paused at the door. It was late, he'd talked his way into being able to see her since visiting hours had finished over an hour ago.

*Should he knock?*

*Or just go in?*

Quietly he stepped into the room, deciding that if Zoe was sleeping he would leave. She wasn't. The light by her bed was on, and she was looking at a picture.

Zoe looked up. Her face brightened as their eyes locked.

Max rushed over to her. "Are you all right?"

Zoe nodded. He embraced her, enjoying how her arms felt around his neck. She kissed him hard on the lips. It might have only been this morning since he'd farewelled her on the shopping trip, but it felt like a lot longer. Her taste tingled on his lips. It felt great to have her in his arms again.

"The baby?" he asked softly.

"Is fine."

"I'm so glad you're both fine." He kissed her again. "Don't think I'm letting you out of my sight again."

"You'll get sick of me."

"I won't."

She rested her head on his chest. "I did something."

Max didn't like the tone of her voice. "You'll have to be more specific."

"I..." She sighed. "I had to have a scan... of the baby... and, well... everything is fine, but... I couldn't resist finding out... the gender."

"Well, don't tell me."

"Mom was with me."

"So, then both of you will have to be good at keeping a secret."

"On that point..."

"Don't tell me, she told my mom."

"And your sister."

He sighed with disappointment. "Do you think you can all manage not to tell me?"

"I have to be honest with you..." Zoe put on a slightly serious face. "... there's no hope. They've already made suggestions on how to decorate the baby's room and you'll find out I have no doubt."

"I must say—"

Zoe put her finger on his lips and silenced him. "You weren't here."

Her words cut deeply. *I wasn't. I was trying to give you a surprise.* He still was trying.

It was taking all of his self-control not to tell her right now. He wanted it to be a surprise when she got back to the farm. And the cattle were still to be sold, and he wanted to give her a solid figure of how much she had to spend.

*Maybe this is the price I pay for the surprise.*

He was disappointed not to have been with her. But then the cattle could've been sold a day later, or a week later, or next month even. The satellite dish could've waited, in all honesty.

*I have to readjust my expectations.* This was something he didn't do well. But he had to. For the sake of the baby, and for Zoe.

"Tell me."

"We are having a baby girl."

He grinned. The words that squeezed his heart was 'we are.' He felt even more connected with Zoe than ever before.

Max kissed her. "I'm so glad *we are.*"

"Look." Zoe handed him the photo she'd been looking at. "Our first baby picture."

"She's beautiful."

"You can make out her face... just." Zoe pointed to the image.

He could see it. Their baby. He was going to be a

dad. His stomach roiled. *What sort of dad was he going to be if he was too busy working on the farm?*

"We need to come up with some names for a baby girl," said Zoe.

"You've got a few suggestions?"

Zoe nodded, grinning secretively at him. She glowed. What people said about pregnant women blossoming was true. Instead of being annoyed. He'd missed seeing the baby for the first time with Zoe, but her happiness was infectious. If he was going to be frustrated with anyone, he knew that person had to be himself. It wasn't going to be as simple as Zoe moving in, giving her some money to do up the house and the room for the baby, he needed to change too.

Max sat on the bed, next to Zoe, stretched his legs out over the top of the sheets. She snuggled into him, her head resting on his chest. He put his right arm around Zoe, and held her close, while they looked at the photo.

"Do you think the name Isla might suit her?" asked Max. "

"Not close to what I was thinking, but I like it."

"I do, too. I saw it once in my family tree. I think it was my great, great, great, great, grandma's name."

"I'll add it to the list."

"And where are you keeping that list?" He raised an eyebrow at her. "Somewhere reliable, I hope."

"Of course." She pretended to look surprised. "In my head, it's a very reliable place."

He chuckled softly. "What's your top name."

"Harper."

"You've been thinking of names then?"

"I had to do something to pass the time."

"I'm sorry I wasn't here." Max felt like he'd be apologizing for the next few months over this one.

"That's fine. I know there will be times when you have to do things on the farm."

"Not when I'm going to miss out."

"I didn't plan for everyone to find out."

"I'll just have to be around more." He believed her. "I like the name Harper by the way."

"Can I ask you something?"

"Of course." The change in the tone of her voice set him on edge.

"How do you cope with being on the farm by yourself for so long?"

He shrugged. "It's the only life I've known, I guess."

"That's all?"

Max rubbed his chin with his left hand. "I have a lot of jobs to do, I think that helps. And when I feel lonely then I go into Burra and see my mates." He could guess why she was asking.

"You know you can invite your friends Ellie and Billie over to stay. I think Billie might be doing a shearing run, up at Burra in late January, maybe she can stay then?"

"I'll ask her." She glanced up at him. "You think you'll cope with two women in the house?"

"If not, I'll go into town and see my friends and stay the night." He kissed her forehead, enjoying how she leaned into him.

"You're not feeling too lonely?"

She exhaled heavily.

He sensed there was a lot of emotion behind her sigh. "You'll get to know some of the locals more."

"How?"

This was something he needed to ask his mom or sister. For him it was a bit different because of the farm. "Maybe we can go to the pub for a meal more often."

"I think I need to do more than that."

"You have a baby to grow first."

"I can multi-task, you know?"

"Okay, well... I don't know what else to suggest. I know you'll figure something out. Don't you have some legal research to do?"

"There's been a little work, but it's slowing down in the lead up to Christmas. And I'm worried there won't be much work next year."

"Don't worry about next year, it will take care of itself." He mused at what he'd just said. It was something his dad used to say to him. Maybe Zoe and I are more suited to each other than we realized.

"There's a lot to do for Christmas first," added Max.

"On that note..."

Max had a sudden awareness that there had been a lot of planning today between his mom and Leanne.

"Don't tell me, it's all be organized between our moms."

"Something like that. The lunch got a bit heated."

"Is that what caused you to end up in the hospital?" He braced himself. If needed he would talk to his mom and tell her to give Zoe some space.

"I like to think not. It's all fine now. Everyone is learning to get along."

"I'll chat with mom, if you want me to."

Zoe shook her head. "They've agreed about what to cook for the family meal on Christmas day."

"That's a miracle in itself." Max couldn't help berating himself for not being there today for Zoe. *I'll do better.*

"It was."

"Sounds like you handled the situation well."

"I want to make sure that you're fine with the arrangement for Christmas, too."

"What do you mean?"

"It's the first big event for us as a couple. I want us to decide on what *we* want."

Max hadn't thought about this Christmas like that. He'd been more focussed on trying to make Zoe comfortable, and even then, he might've missed the mark. He didn't like the fact that she was feeling lonely on the farm. If Ellie or Billie could come and visit her even for a few days, he was sure that would help. Both were farm girls and used to the wide-open spaces and life on a farm.

"I want whatever will make you happy." She'd given up her life in the city to come and live with him, and he wanted to accommodate her to make up for how much she'd given up. She'd resigned from her job, moved away from her family and friends, it was the least he could do.

"What would make me happy is both of us deciding on what we want for Christmas. It's our first Christmas together, and I want it to be special."

"It will be." He squeezed her closer to him.

"Max."

He paused, hearing his name in that tone made him realize he wasn't listening to her. "Having you with me is my priority for Christmas," he said softly, finally allowing himself to voice what he wanted. "Maybe breakfast together, just us, then my family and your family can come over. But that would be hard if your family is staying with us, which they can by the way."

Zoe looked at him and grinned.

"I gave the right answer?" He'd been speaking from his heart.

She rolled her eyes. "Max, there's no right or wrong answer. I want to discuss this with you, so it's *our* decision."

His stomach flipped at the thought.

*Our decision.*

They were a couple.

Ordinarily they would've decided together on when starting a family, but they had jumped ahead on that one. They had decided on living together and seeing how things went. He guessed this was the next decision they needed to make together.

"I like the sound of breakfast together on Christmas Day, but I would like my parents to stay with us."

"Hmmm… maybe they could stay with my mom for a few days, then come to the farm Christmas Day."

"That might work."

"I feel you're going to say a but."

"But the food needs to be started early."

"Easily fixed. How about we have an early breakfast?"

"No sleep in?"

"Sleep in and no breakfast, or no sleep in and an early breakfast."

"Tough decisions." She grinned. "Let's sleep in."

"So, let your parents stay with us then?"

"Yes. We can have breakfast together any day." Zoe settled back down on his chest, trying to suppress a yawn.

"You should get some sleep."

"Hmmm… I will. Now you're here."

Max kissed her gently on the top of her head. "Sweet dreams."

Things were going to have to change big time, and it was him that was going to have to make the adjustments. It was going to need to be more than making sure there was money and the internet connection. He took a deep breath, trying to settle the rising concern he was feeling.

Zoe began to feel heavier next to him on the bed as she fell asleep. The blurry image in his mind, kept him awake. Thinking. Wondering. Trying to make some plans that would mean he would be around for Zoe and their baby girl.

It was challenging to think of what to do when he had no idea what to expect with a baby on the way.

# CHAPTER 8

**THURSDAY 5TH DECEMBER**

"I can't wait to come up to see you at Christmas," said her mom.

Her mom and dad had met them for brunch after Zoe had been discharged from the hospital. Max was driving her back to Greenfields today. The ute was packed, full of new outfits for her to wear, nothing flash but all very practical, and she was happy about that. There were also a few things for the baby, each grandma-to-be couldn't resist buying. Helen and Kate had gone back to the Burra yesterday, so they could take care of the few jobs at the farm until Max and Zoe arrived. Zoe was so glad she'd been given the all-clear this morning to go home. She couldn't believe how much she was thinking Greenfields was now her home.

"Me, too," Zoe gave her mom a long hug goodbye.

"You take care," said her dad, joining in the family hug.

"Of course." She wasn't sure why people kept saying that to her. She didn't do much in her day compared to when working as a legal secretary, and it was starting to drive her a bit crazy having so much spare time. It didn't help with the thoughts, or with the emotions. She been given medication for her low blood pressure, and had a series of follow up appointments with the doctors at Burra over Christmas and the New Year, and then she was going to be coming back next Thursday to the Women's and Children's Hospital to see Dr. Khatri, who was now taking charge of the medical side of her pregnancy. Zoe was trying to see the positive side of having to come to Adelaide each month until the baby was born. At least, she'd get to see her parents more, and some of her friends.

*I won't be feeling so lonely then.*

Zoe was glad she'd spoken to Max about how she was feeling. He had jobs to keep him busy all day. Decorating the baby's room would keep her occupied for only so long. With the help of her mom, Helen and Kate, she knew the basics had been covered. Zoe needed something else, and her mom's words to find a hobby kept circling in her mind.

*What sort of hobby could she do?* Knitting wasn't her thing, or painting or drawing. She liked to read books but did enough of that already. Hiking wasn't her style either. She couldn't go horse riding. She needed something more dynamic but had no idea of what that could be.

"I'll see you in a few weeks." She got into the ute, and Max closed the door for her.

"I'm so glad we got to meet you again," said her mom as she hugged him good-bye.

"You're going to see me a lot more, you know," said Max.

"And we're very happy about that."

Zoe raised her eyebrows. She'd quizzed Max to see if her mom had decided to talk to him about not initially coming down to Adelaide with her. He assured her she hadn't. Zoe wasn't so sure.

Max turned and shook her dad's hand. "I'll see you later."

"Take good care of my daughter and grand-daughter."

"Of course."

Max got into the driver's seat and started the engine.

Zoe extended her hand out of the open window and waved as the car pulled away. Her eyes watered, but this time she let the tears fall.

\*\*\*

. . .

Zoe smiled as the ute turned into the driveway for Greenfields. *Home.* It was as if being away for a few days, and returning now, caused her to see the farm for the first time.

Soft rolling hills surrounded them, making a nice change from viewing flat land for the last few hours. A few eucalyptus and tea-trees lined either side of the driveway. The grass brown already from the start of summer, the dry land showing its own unique beauty. The old house, built by Max's ancestors, stood proudly on a rise, as if waiting for them.

Surrounded by a brick fence on one side, and a corrugated iron fence on the other sides, the boundaries of home were clearly defined. It had a metal roof, angular to let the rain runoff into the gutters to be collected in their water tanks, which were huge and on the other side of the house. She hoped to be able to hear the rain falling on it come winter. The house was large, four bedrooms to house growing families. The thought caused her to place her hand on her belly, to which she was rewarded with a flutter from baby.

A few old corrugated iron sheds came into view beyond the house. Some of them housed farm machinery, the others simply held the tools of Max's father, and grandfather, even great grandfather, in a mess of dust and cobwebs. She'd only poked her head to see once, sneezed, then left not interested in exploring the shadows within. Now, her curiosity spiked. She might like to have a closer look in the sheds, to explore and learn more about Max's heritage. She was going to have the time.

The doctor had made it clear she needed to rest. A lot. She didn't tell the doctor she wasn't that sort of person. She figured that looking through the sheds wouldn't be taxing on her or put the baby in any sort of danger.

In between them was the hen house, the black hens were out scratching around in the dry dirt finding seeds to eat. To the right was the dog kennels, but she was too far away to see if Snipper was there.

A big ghost gum stood outside of the house yard, momentarily blocking the view of the house as they approached. Its old branches stretched out providing shade to the side of the house. A wide trunk, ghostly gray in color, offered a sense of stability.

Zoe wound down the window, letting the hot afternoon air into the ute. She breathed in, enjoying the fresh country air. A mix of earthiness, animals, and the fresh scent of eucalyptus filled her lungs. It felt good. Right. To be here, with Max, a subtle reassurance she hadn't thought she'd needed.

Max drove slowly around the ghost gum, to the back of the house, stopping by the gate of the house yard. "Glad to be back," Max glanced at her.

"To be home with you, yes." She smiled at him, reached out and placed a hand on his leg, his body warmth seeping into her palm in a comforting sensation. They may have left separately, but they were coming home together.

"I'm glad you think this is your home." His grin was broad, causing his eyes to sparkle.

Bluey ran out to greet them, his tail wagging madly.

"Now that's a good welcome," said Zoe laughing at how excited the dog was to see them.

"Hey, what's that on the roof?" Zoe pointed as Max unbuckled his seat belt.

He turned and grinned at her.

"Oh, is that's why you couldn't come with me to Adelaide? You were putting up the satellite dish?" It was starting to make a bit more sense now. She'd thought Max wanted to commit to her and their baby, but the doubt had grown with him not coming with her to Adelaide whether she wanted to admit that or not.

"And something else."

Zoe looked at him curious to hear what he had to say. She couldn't think what it might be that he'd been working on.

"And here I thought you were just working hard out on the farm."

"I am." He grinned. "I sold a herd of cattle. I received the call today, and I got a great price considering it's right before Christmas and the market has been low."

"That is great news." She knew they needed the

money with the baby on the way, and now extra trips to Adelaide to see her obstetrician things were going to get expensive very quickly.

"The money is for you."

"Thanks, but I don't mind making do, your house is more than functional as it is. And I only need some paint for the baby's room. Mom's getting new curtains made, and your mom is buying new carpet." Honestly, they needed to spend money on other things—renovating the house was a luxury they couldn't afford right now.

"I don't want you to make do."

"How much is a herd of cattle worth?"

"It was only a small herd." He moved restlessly in the ute seat as if getting irritated with the discussion they were having.

"Paint doesn't cost that much," Zoe said softly. "I'm very good with money, I can make it go further with some careful planning."

"It will be over twenty grand."

*Shit.* Her eyes widened as her breath caught in her throat. That was a lot of money.

"For what?" she managed to ask when she found her voice. They didn't need a nursery that was going to cost that amount of money.

"To help make the house yours. You know, to do what you women do."

"Which is…?" She had to settle herself. He was a

bachelor, older than her, and had some odd views about what women should do. Luckily, she was good at setting him straight.

"Decorate," he said hesitantly.

*He's trying. Doing only what he knows*, she reminded herself.

"That's very generous of you." Her mind whirled. *What the hell was she going to do with that money?* No one had given her that amount of money in her life. Not even her parents.

"You think it's a good idea then? You don't seem to be as happy with getting that amount of money as I thought you would be."

"I'm blown away."

"In a good way?"

She took a deep breath and nodded. "I don't need that much money. We need to spend it on the farm, don't we?"

"Yes. But you've given up so much to move here, for us, for the baby, for our family-to-be. I don't want you to be lonely, or uncomfortable here."

She wanted to say she wasn't. But what he said was true. Being here alone was difficult, more so than she ever thought possible.

She knew one thing, though. "Money won't fix those feelings I have."

"It might help ease them, though," he shot back.

She could tell he'd put a lot of thought into this.

And here she was almost rejecting his gift. That was the last thing she wanted to be doing.

"Okay, so you know what? I think I can make a list of what could be replaced in the house, and we can discuss what can be changed now, and what can wait. I'd like to spend the money together."

"I'm happy to go with whatever you decide."

Max was such a bachelor. A typical working man who was happy to leave the house side of things to his partner. She was surprised there were men who still thought like that these days, though he was that bit older than her.

"No, we decide this together or I won't spend a cent." She glared at him, enforcing her point of view.

"You're not going to budge on this one, are you?"

"No. This is your money."

"And I'm giving it to you... to make the house yours."

"I want the house to be *ours*."

There was a glint in his eyes, as if he finally got what she was trying to tell him. He might not want to think about things which were house-related, but he had to if they were going to make it theirs.

"Okay."

"Okay what?"

He smiled at her. His eyes sparkling with a new look on life. "I'll help you work out what needs to be changed in the house, and this will be *our* home, for *our* baby."

Her eyes welled with tears. "Thank you."

Max leaned over and kissed her, his lips sweet on hers, and she felt herself getting lost with him as they connected on a deeper level.

This was a very big step forward, and she was so glad he was by her side, and they were taking it together.

# CHAPTER 9

MONDAY 9TH DECEMBER

Zoe slipped into one of the new dresses bought last week. It was a blue stretch material, firm over her growing bust line, low cut, and short full skirt. Barely nine o'clock in the morning and the day was already feeling hot. Due to the constant reminder from Max, she'd been taking the last few days easy. She didn't want to faint again and end up in the hospital. Now, she was bored, and it was time to do something other than sitting around the house all day. They'd made some progress with their list of changes to the home, and she needed a break from that activity.

Max was out on the farm, checking the water again. This time she decided not to go with him. In an attempt to get to know his family better, she'd rung Kate, who had the day off of work at the local agricultural store and she had agreed to come and take her into Burra for brunch.

Zoe had to admit, she was looking forward to the outing. Ready, well ahead of time, she decided to wander outside instead of waiting indoors.

The warm breeze was a delight on her bare legs as she stepped outside, the screen door banging shut behind her. She looked out, considering what she wanted to do. The eggs were already collected for the morning, and the hens were clucking around the yard, scratching at the dirt and pecking at insects.

The clothesline was to her right in the house yard, also the water tanks, and the land then extended out into paddocks where the cattle roamed. There was nothing to explore in that direction. To her left was the ghost gum tree standing stoic in the heat. She rubbed her belly, spying the sheds. They called to her. For a moment, she decided to put on boots, but then not wanting to bother, she walked out in her brown sandals.

*I'll make some noise that will scare away any snakes.*

Thumping her feet on the ground, and stirring up small dust clouds, she wandered down to the sheds. She went into the closest one first, pulling hard on the creaky door to force the rusted hinges to move.

"Ahchoo." Zoe sneezed from the dust in the air.

Sunlight filtered into the dark space of the shed, dust particles dancing in the rays as she walked in further. A huge, thick wooden work table sat in the middle of the shed, old tools scattered on top which were covered in decades of dust. On the far wall, there was a narrow workbench, full of more tools, and up to the roof there was box shelving with even more tools inside.

To the right, she noticed a pile of wood. Curious she walked closer. It wasn't just one type of wood, there were planks from a variety of trees, cut and dry, but somehow she knew they weren't for firewood. The wood seemed more precious.

She glanced back at the tools and picked one up. She'd worked enough with her dad in his shed over the years to know this was a plane. It was old, dusty, and needed a good clean, but it still could be used. An idea seeded in her mind. There were chisels on the table, in good condition, at least they would be after a serious clean and some oil.

Zoe turned around looking at the shed with fresh insight. This had been someone's workspace for wood carving. She wondered who. Max's grandpa? Father? She was curious. She wanted to find out more. The idea grew in her mind.

She had enjoyed helping her dad with the jobs around the house and had a basic idea of how to use tools. These were old and not powered with electricity, which appealed to her even more.

Zoe was going to have to do some more research, see if this was something she could do. Based on the way her skin prickled, and how much happier she simply felt at this potential idea, she was sure it would work out. For one, she didn't have to spend any money, there were plenty of tools to use, and there was even a substantial supply of wood. All that was needed to be done was to clean up the years of dust and cobwebs and do some research online.

*I think I've just found my hobby.* But would Max let her use these tools. Let alone do something like wood carving.

The sound of a vehicle approaching broke through her thoughts, and she stepped out to see Kate parking the SVU near the ghost gum. Zoe waved, pulled the door closed, and walked up to her.

"Whatcha doing in the shed?" asked Kate as Zoe slid into the SVU, slamming the door closed, and buckling up her seatbelt.

"I was curious. Who did the wood carving tools belong to?"

Kate reversed the SVU, did a U-turn and started back along the driveway. "Grandpa. Dad and Max weren't into wood carving."

"Or you?"

"No, it didn't interest me either. So, they just sat there in the shed where he left them. I've never really thought about it." Kate turned on to the main road which would take them into Burra.

"Do you have any of the pieces your grandpa made?"

"Hmmm... I have a small bowl he made with me

before he passed. I was about eight. I have it by my bed for my jewelry."

"He was skilled at it?"

"Yeah, he sold most of his pieces, and didn't keep much of what he made."

Zoe was impressed.

*Could I do something like that?* The idea just kept growing in her mind.

It could be a source of income.

*Would I be any good?*

"Do you think it would be all right if I used his tools?"

"I don't see why not." Kate kept her eyes focussed on the road.

"Do you think Max would mind?" asked Zoe. Something told her that he might not really like the idea of her using tools in the shed.

"I wouldn't tell him."

Zoe laughed. "You wouldn't?"

"Nope. But don't you dare tell him I told you that."

"As long as you don't tell him, I'm going to do wood carving."

"You're serious?"

"I think so. I'll need to do some research first, and it will take a bit of effort to clean up the shed. I need a hobby, and well, it feels exciting to give this a try."

"I'll come and help you clean up the shed if you like. Just let me know."

"Thanks, I will." Zoe smiled to herself as they

approached Burra, and the open paddocks were slowly being replaced by more houses.

Kate parked the car in front of the café, Bits and Bobs. Zoe had eaten there before and thought it quaint. Now, looking in at the café with her hobby in mind, another idea came to her. The café was also a second-hand gift store. If it worked out, and if she could produce quality carvings, she might well have a local place to try and sell her pieces.

Things were finally coming together, her new life in the country, and it was blossoming with potential.

# CHAPTER 10

**THURSDAY 12TH DECEMBER**

"Are you ready?" asked Zoe as Max strode up the path toward the house. She sat outside sitting at the wrought iron round table under the veranda. Her cell in hand, she'd been searching videos to give her ideas of how to start up wood carving.

She hadn't told Max yet, that was something she was planning to do. It wasn't like it was dangerous, not really, not if she was careful. She was going to take on Kate's advice, and not tell him. At least, not yet. She was hatching a very big plan, and with Christmas approaching, there wasn't a lot of time to implement what she really wanted to do.

"I'll wash up first, and change clothes." Max stopped and kissed her, leaving her mouth on fire with passion as he went inside.

Zoe stayed outside, searching for more videos on wood carving. She had no plans to tackling anything too challenging to start with. She wanted to create more practical items, things which didn't cost a lot of money so they could be sold.

Yesterday, Kate had come over once Max had gone out on the farm to fix a fence, and they'd cleaned the shed. It had been an enormous task, and she was glad Kate was there to help out. On the outside of the shed, there was no indication of the change that had happened inside.

Max had thought that she was spending time with his sister, which he was pleased about, and in a way she was. It was just that Kate was helping her to do something that he might not really want her to do.

Inside the shed, the tools were now organized on the narrow workbench that ran the length of the wall. The thick layer of dust was removed—there were no cobwebs, well, there might be now—and it was ready for her to use. All Zoe needed to do was to decide on the first project. She was nearly ready to start her new hobby, and she couldn't be happier. That and the fact that Max was coming with her to the doctor's check-up today. In Adelaide.

Max came out, dressed in clean jeans, and a polo shirt. "I'm ready?"

She slipped her cell into her handbag and stood. Zoe took his hand in hers, enjoying the glow of happiness in his eyes, as they walked to the ute together.

"Let's go see this baby together."

***

Max stood nervously next to Zoe as she lay on the bed, her belly exposed while the doctor moved the probe through an excess of gel spread over her stomach. The screen flashed between dark shadows and light, and he couldn't make out anything. Somewhere on the screen was an image of their baby. He couldn't wait to see it in the moment for the first time, since he'd missed out last week when Zoe was in hospital.

He'd noticed a change in Zoe these last few days. It wasn't as if she hadn't been making an effort before, but things had been different. She'd caught up with Kate more than once, and it made him relieved and happy she was getting to know his family and not spending so much time alone. They'd had a family lunch on Sunday.

After this meeting with the doctor, he was going to have afternoon tea with Zoe's mom and dad. He surprised himself that he felt calm about that, and was more nervous now, about seeing the baby and if all was well.

"There we go," said Dr. Khatri. "There's your baby." She clicked some buttons and took some measurements.

Max stared at the screen. He felt his eyes begin to water. This was real. His baby, their baby, was up on the screen.

*Was she doing all right?*

He felt Zoe squeeze his hand. Looking at her, his heart melted. She was amazing, lying there as if this was normal.

*It is normal,* he tried to tell himself.

This was nerve-wracking for him. He'd much prefer to help a cow birth a calf, he knew what to expect then. Now he felt completely out of his comfort zone. Though, at the same time, he didn't want to miss another second of this journey with Zoe. This meant the world to him, to be with her, that she trusted him enough to let him be there even though they were still very much getting to know each other.

"Relax, everything's going well," said Dr. Khatri. "The nurse tells me your blood pressure has stabilized which is good news."

"So, I don't have to see you for a while?" asked Zoe.

"Nice try," said Dr, Khatri with a smile. "You'll have to keep all the appointments, but you can start to do a little more, but not too much. And don't overdo it over Christmas."

"Great." Zoe grinned, and squeezed Max's hand. "Did you hear that?" She looked at him cheekily.

"Yes, you can't overdo it. I'll check with my mom and your mom, and we will have Christmas covered. You won't need to do anything."

"That sounds boring," said Zoe.

"That sounds more like Max is looking out for you very well," Dr. Khatri interjected.

Max smiled. "I'm glad I'm doing something right."

"You're doing a lot right," said Zoe reassuringly.

"I'll print some photos for you, and I'll see you both in the New Year."

"Great," said Zoe, wiping the gel from her belly.

Max helped her sit and to get off the bed. He couldn't help it, he hugged her tightly.

"What was that for?" asked Zoe, her face alight with a broad grin.

It was a relief for both of them that the pregnancy was back on track.

"Because I love you."

He enjoyed seeing her blush.

"I love you, too." She wrapped her arms around his waist and hugged him into her.

"This is going to be a great Christmas with you," he whispered.

"And baby." Zoe winked.

"And baby." He rested his hand on her belly.

The baby kicked.

He grinned.

Not planned, but it was the best thing that could have happened to have Zoe and their baby in his life.

He couldn't wait to meet their baby girl and start really being a dad.

# CHAPTER 11

WEDNESDAY 25TH DECEMBER, CHRISTMAS
DAY

Zoe couldn't believe she'd kept her wood carving a
secret over the last few weeks. And now, there was
going to be a big reveal. Helen and Leanne had taken
over the kitchen, the roast was on, and the smell was
making her hungry even though she'd only had breakfast not that long ago.

They all sat in the lounge room, Kate and Helen,
and her parents Leanne and Robert. After a discussion
with Max last night, they'd gone out and chosen a small
branch from the ghost gum outside and brought it
inside to decorate as their Christmas tree. Zoe had
purchased a string of led lights and strung them
between the leaves, and they spent a little time adding a

few baubles. It was simple, perfect, and reflected them. Zoe felt that this was the start of a new tradition and teared up knowing that next year they would have a little girl with them to share this joy.

"How long until the food is ready," asked Robert.

"You've just had breakfast. You can't be hungry already," answered Leanne.

"It's Christmas… I'll be hungry all day," he grinned broadly.

"I want to give you my gifts first," said Zoe. She was glad that this time with both sides of the family together, there had been no sign of any augments starting.

She got up and handed out the presents she'd wrapped yesterday in secret. Finally, she'd found a hobby. The wood carving was turning out to be a good way for her to keep active, but also to relax. It had been a push to finish before Christmas, but she'd managed to make something for everyone.

"Wow! They're heavy," said her mom.

"I made them myself." She handed the last one to Max, her belly a flutter of nerves. He was about to find out what she'd been hiding from him for the previous few weeks. She sat next to him on the arm of the single lounge chair he was sitting in.

"You're very clever to make your own gifts," said Helen.

"Go on, open them," said Zoe, holding her breath at the sound of Christmas paper ripping.

"Wow," said Robert. He turned a small bowl over in his hand.

"For your loose change, Dad," said Zoe. She had to keep the designs simple while she learned her skills.

"You made this?" asked Helen, while she held up a large wooden cutting board made from two types of wood, pine and jarrah. That was something else Zoe had learned in the last few weeks, the type of wood that was in the shed Max's grandpa had found.

"I don't believe it," said her mom, holding up a similar wooden cutting board. "I don't know that you should be doing thi—"

"Leanne, I think our daughter has done an amazing job," interrupted Robert.

"But she could've hurt herself."

"She hasn't," said her dad sternly.

"You said I needed a hobby, Mom," said Zoe. "And after finding the wood carving tools in the shed... well, what can I say? I love my new hobby."

"And, so you should," said her dad with a smile. "This is great."

"I think this is awesome, and you've come along so quickly," said Kate holding up a set of small spoons.

"Hang on, sounds like you knew about this," Max said to Kate.

"I... um... well, yes."

Zoe wasn't sure if the look of surprise on Max's face was good or not.

Max sighed.

"I think you could sell these," said Helen.

"Thanks, I hope to get good enough to sell them online. And, when I'm ready, Elly at Bits and Bobs said I can sell some in the café in Burra."

"That's great," praised her dad.

"It won't be a high income, but I hope it will be something given time," said Zoe. She twisted her hands together, not liking that Max hadn't said anything.

"Do you like it?" she asked softly, unsure if she really wanted to hear his answer.

"No."

Her heart tightened.

He took her hand in his and squeezed. "I love it. Like I love you."

Her eyes misted. "Cheeky bastard." She giggled, the emotion bubbling inside of her.

Max picked up the wooden item which was the hardest thing she'd made. A cut out of a Christmas tree, sanded and polished in jarrah wood. It was a stencil she'd found in the shed that his grandma must have made, that she'd used as a guide.

"Our first real ornament," he added.

"Yes."

"The first of many."

She nodded. "I hope so."

"I know so." He stood up and went over and hung it on the Christmas tree. "It's perfect."

"You don't mind that I've used the tools in the shed?" she asked as he came back over to her.

"I mind that my sister was in on this."

"You'll get over it, bro," said Kate.

"Hmmm..." He gave her a mock stare, before turning to look at Zoe. "I want my home to be your home."

"*Our* home," corrected Zoe.

"*Our* home," echoed Max. "And you've done just that."

"So, you're okay with this?"

"I've just got one thing to say."

Zoe held her breath.

*Good or bad?* She wasn't sure.

The baby fluttered in her belly.

Max put his hand on her stomach and looked in Zoe's eyes. She shivered, feeling the connection strong between them.

"I love you."

Zoe blushed, leaned in, and kissed him. "I love you, too."

"I can't wait to have Christmas with you and our little girl next year. And to see what else you create in the year to come."

"Me, too." Zoe smiled then rested her head on his chest.

"I hope you enjoy your first country Christmas," said Max.

She looked at him in the eyes, the connection strengthening between them. "It's perfect."

The End

If you enjoyed this story, you may also like:

Enjoy more rural romances
By Lilliana Rose
The Royal Show Affair
A Farmer's Christmas

Chasing Dust Clouds
Click here to purchase
A Dusty Christmas
Click here to purchase

Like urban paranormal romance?
Check out these books by Lilliana Rose
Protector Wolf Shifter Series
Bk1: Shadow Wolf
Bk2: Marked Wolf
Bk3: Rogue Wolf

Dragon Bond
Dragon Reborn
Witch Moon Series
Bk1: Dark Moon Secrets

# ACKNOWLEDGMENTS

Thank you Kaylene for editing and always having time to offer support and advice.

Thanks to my sisters for their support of their crazy sister who is a writer, and my toddler boy for being well-behaved so I can still have time to write and nurture my soul.

Thanks to my dog Kimba, for reminding me when it's time to eat and to go to bed, and for simply just lying there next to me or at my feet, being that extra life in the room, so the writing journey isn't so lonely.

# ABOUT THE AUTHOR

Lilliana writes in contemporary romance. She grew up on a sheep farm in Australia, then swapped her workbooks for city heels, and now lives in the city. She enjoys drawing on the contrast between country and city life in the contemporary romance she writes. For her moving to the city was like coming to a different country.

Check out more of her work at www.lillianarose.com Connect with Lilliana Rose on social media.